Veda

A novel

Ellen Gardner

DEDICATION

I dedicate this book to my daughter Stefanie, who never got the chance to know her grandmother.

ACKNOWLEDGMENTS

I want to acknowledge everyone who has helped me in this process. Most especially my six wonderful siblings whose brains I have been picking for years. While our memories have sometimes differed, their input has been invaluable. Second, I owe an immeasurable debt to the people in my critique group who have challenged me, encouraged me, and stretched me every step of the way: Dorothy Vogel, B K Showalter, Dolores de Leon, Addie Greene, Sonja Ferrera, Patricia Florin, Marilyn Joy, Mary Brubaker, Melissa Brown, Gloria Boyd, and Deborah Rothschild. Third, I want to thank my wonderful husband for his years of tireless listening and support.

NOVEMBER 2002

HE LOOKS NATURAL ENOUGH except for the lipstick. At ninety, his once handsome face is still remarkably smooth, but the undertaker has touched it up and added color to his lips. My dad, who railed against such vanities his whole life, is going to meet his maker wearing lipstick.

He had made his own arrangements, leaving detailed instructions on the table in his room, naming the organist, the soloist, the songs, and the pallbearers. And he wrote his obituary, stating date and place of birth, his vocation as a gardener and orchard worker, his religious affiliation, his work as canvasser, soloist, Sabbath School teacher, and deacon. He named his second wife and his third, the dates of their marriages, and the dates each of them passed away. He listed his four children as survivors, but there is no mention of his first wife, his children's mother.

The sanctuary at the small Seventh-day Adventist church is plain. A floral spray with "Father and Grandfather" in gold lettering sits atop the casket, and a couple of small bouquets stand on a table next to the organ. The room is nearly full.

I stare ahead wondering what these folks are thinking about me and my siblings. Most of them have known Daddy for years and have never seen his children.

The minister quotes from the Bible, reads the obituary, and begins his eulogy. "Raymond was an extraordinary man," he says. "...a faithful servant of the Lord...no one was better acquainted with the Bible..." Winding up, he invites people to share their memories. Many stand to express admiration for Raymond's hardiness, his sincerity, and his "unfailing dedication to bringing souls to the Lord."

I hear behind me, "Amen, Amen."

Someone lauds his humility, his steadfast rejection of worldly values.

"Amen, Amen."

My sister speaks of his remarkable memory, and I mention the diaries we found among his things in which he had recorded the weather for more than sixty years.

The soloist sings in a tremulous voice, there is a final prayer, and we file past the casket for a last goodbye. Daddy's only living brother, an uncle we never knew, shakes our hands. We receive condolences, are enveloped in weepy embraces, and are herded into a hall, where a vegetarian lunch has been laid. We are ill at ease in our father's world.

At the cemetery I stand shivering, wishing I could cry. When I was a child, he was the daddy we rarely saw, the daddy whose visits sent Mom into a tailspin. The daddy who never sent money, who scolded us for singing "unchristian" songs or twirling in our dresses. As an adult, I suffered his tedious letters and pleas that I return to the church I was born into. And when, in his last years, I helped him with moving, medications, and paperwork, it wasn't without some amount of resentment.

But the diaries he left fascinated me, and it was reading them that made me decide to write this book. He gave so much attention to the weather and so little to his wife and children. I longed to know more of my mother's story, and ironically, it was between the lines in those cryptic little books that I found it.

I can hear her voice in my head. The way she talked, the way she laughed, how she sounded when she was angry. And I can still hear her singing, off key, the hymns she loved so much.

Veda

1

ME AND MY TWIN SISTER was so little when we were born they put us in shoeboxes behind the woodstove to keep us warm. Scrawny and ugly like a couple of barn rats, was how my brother Laird said it. They give us twin names, Veda and Vida, but they weren't sure which one of us was which. What's important to know is one of us died, and the one that lived, that's me, ended up bein called Veda.

Vida got buried out back of our house, and when I was big enough, I went out there and talked to her. Told her I wished she would of lived so I could have somebody to play with instead of just Laird, who was a boy and didn't even know how to hold a baby doll except for by its feet.

Mama had a whole bunch of other kids before we got born, so she was pretty wore out. My oldest sister, Bea, was already eighteen and fixin to git married, and there was Wilbert and George and Lettie and Zelda, all the way down to Laird, who was four. And there was two other ones besides my twin that died. Papa was twenty years older'n Mama and he was wore out too, but not for the same reason. He was a cowboy before he met Mama and had got done in by all the ropin and ridin. But accordin to Mama he got off easy. She said if he was the one havin the babies, there wouldn't never been more'n one.

He'd come from a big family, too, and like me he was the youngest. When his ma got old and sick, he was the one that took care of her and the family ranch. That's why she left it to him. Once he found himself in charge of that big old place, he figured he better git a wife and start raisin his own crop of kids to help him run it. Said he picked Mama 'cause she was a spitfire and he liked that about her.

I was crazy about my Papa. He had white hair and whiskers and a wrinkly face. Had a horse fall on him once that broke his leg so he had this funny, tip-to-the-left way of walkin that made it easy to pick him out from a mile off. But even old and crippled up, he was a hard worker. And Papa had this way about him — always teasin and jokin and cuttin up — that made Mama mad when he done it but always made me laugh.

Anyways that's where I was born, in 19-and-18, on that ranch near John Day, Oregon. I would of grew up there, too, except for Papa goin crazy. He been workin on Mama for a long time to let him sell the place. Said he was sick of it and wanted to go somewhere else. Mama told him she wasn't leavin, that the ranch had give em a decent livin, and it still would if he would just settle down. But he kept on pesterin her over it and wouldn't let it alone. She stood her ground right up to when Papa threw his big fit.

What he done was, he went out one mornin and dragged all his tools out of the barn and piled em up.

Harrows, hay rakes, saddles, sheep shears, and he threw in a half dozen or so hay bales to boot. Then he drove his new John Deere tractor into the middle of it and climbed up on its nose. Stood there all wild-haired and red-faced and commenced to rantin. Said he was fixin to set the whole goddamn mess afire and himself with it. Mama yelled at him and called him a damn fool and cried out to God for help. But that was what done it. That's what made her give in.

Papa got word of a place for sale out in the Rogue Valley of southwest Oregon and bought it without even goin to look. Sold our ranch and ever'thin that went with it, includin most of the livestock and his new tractor. Then he told Mama what he done and said to pack up.

I was about six then and my brother Laird was ten. The others was all grown and not livin at home. Mama didn't want to leave, but she said she'd made a bargain with God, that if God would keep Papa from goin crazy like that again, she'd go wherever she had to.

We must of been a sight, me and Mama in the wagon and Laird and Papa ridin horses, drivin our two milk cows the whole way. Soon as we got moved Mama started lookin for a church. She said church was the only thing that'd kept her goin all those years, and she couldn't settle down till she found one. Problem was, most of em was Sunday churches, and far as she was concerned, goin to church on Sunday was akin to worshippin the devil.

Saturday had always been our church day and it wasn't till I started school that I found out we were different. I didn't understand why we didn't do like everbody else. When I asked Mama, she pulled out her Bible. "It's right here in Genesis," she said, pointin to the place. "God rested on the seventh day, and any fool with a calendar can see that's not Sunday." That didn't really answer my question. But botherin Mama about it only made her cross. Just 'cause other people did somethin, she said, didn't make it right.

Papa didn't take religion serious like Mama did, and she had even less patience with him than she had with me. He was always makin fun. Sayin Seventh-day Adventists were the gloomiest bunch a folks he ever laid eyes on. He even started callin his old cow the Adventist Cow 'cause of how she looked so mournful all the time.

"Miles," Mama scolded, "that's not respectful."

"Oh, I don't know about that," he said. "She don't seem to mind."

"I didn't mean the cow ... and you know it. Adventists are good people and I won't have you talkin that way."

Papa was good natured and, for the most part, went along with Mama's Adventist rules. Except for the ones against meat and coffee. He said neither one of them things had hurt him yet and he wasn't about to give em up. He'd come to breakfast and find Mama standin straddle-legged, fists on her hipbones, ready for a fight.

"Where's my coffee?" he'd ask.

"It's bad for you."

"Where's the bacon? I want bacon with my eggs."

"Pig flesh is unclean. Says so in the Bible."

Mama could be thorny as a rosebush, but in a contest of wills Papa usually won.

2

WE NO MORE'N GOT SETTLED when Papa changed his mind about the place he bought. Said he wanted to start a dairy farm and needed more pasture. That was news to Mama, but she didn't argue. So Papa got his bigger pasture, but then he couldn't afford to buy the cows. We moved again, to still another place in the Rogue Valley, and Mama kept prayin he'd settle down. She said as long as the Lord kept his end of the bargain, she'd keep hers, but she wasn't goin to go to all the trouble of plantin gardens, 'cause she was afraid Papa'd get another bee in his bonnet before they had a chance to grow.

Papa had bragged so much about the Rogue Valley climate that the rest of the family started movin out too. First it was just Bea and her husband, Gabe, then pretty soon Wilbert and George come out, and finally even Lettie and Zelda. Once the whole family was back together, and Mama had found a church, she really didn't want to be movin anymore. Then Papa bought himself a Model T Ford, and that was a real worry to Mama. Partly 'cause she didn't trust his drivin and partly 'cause it give him the chance to look for property farther away.

Even though Mama didn't trust Papa's drivin, we did have to git to church. So ever Saturday Mama told Papa to get the car ready. He'd put down his coffee cup and go outside to the Ford. We'd hear crank, crank, crank, putt, putt, putt, BANG! Crank, crank, crank, putt, putt, putt, BANG, "Goddamn it!" Mama'd go to the door and holler, "Miles! It's the Sabbath!"

Then it'd start over, crank, crank, crank, putt, putt, putt, BANG! After five or six tries, the putt, putt got steady. "She's runnin now," Papa'd yell. "If ya don't come on, you'll be late." Mama'd be so put out at him for usin bad language she wouldn't say a word to him all the way to church.

And what Mama feared happened. Papa traded our place in Evans Creek for one in a little town called Cave Junction, forty miles or so out the Redwood Highway, and Mama didn't dare fight him. So, like all the other times, she said, "We'll just have to make the best of it."

That was the year I turned thirteen and I didn't want to make the best of it. I didn't want to move. I liked my school and my teacher, Miss Hunicutt. I had girlfriends. And there was that red-headed boy, Thomas, that ever since Valentine's Day was sneakin me notes and pieces of candy. I cried so much, Mama said if I didn't quit I'd make myself sick.

"Papa," I begged, "we can't move, not all that way. I don't want to leave. I don't want to go to a different school."

"Well then, that settles it," he said. "You can read and write. That's enough schoolin for a girl. You'll just up and git married anyhow."

"But I'm only thirteen," I cried. "I won't be gittin married for a long time."

Papa didn't answer. Just stood up and hooked his thumbs in his suspenders. "When's supper, Carrie?" he asked, headin for the back door. Mama and me looked at each other. There wasn't much chance I could make Papa change his mind, but I had to try. I followed him out the door.

"Papa," I said, runnin to keep up. "Papa, please."

"It's done, Veda, it's settled. I want you to stay home now. Help your ma. Yer almost grown, it's time you learn somethin practical."

"I'll help Mama more, I promise. And I'll change schools if I have to ... just don't make me quit."

"Nope," he said. "The new place is gonna take a lotta work. Your ma will need you."

Cave Junction wasn't even a real town, and I didn't like it one bit. There was just some small shops and a couple of churches. And it was a good thing for Mama that one of em was Adventist. It was a pretty place, I guess, with the mountains and all, but once you got off the main road it was just forest. And back in the trees, where our house was, the sun almost never got in. It was always cold and damp. And gloomy.

"That hang-dog look won't change anything," Mama was always sayin to me. "Your Pa is right about one thing. You'll be gittin married someday, and you'll need to know how to cook and keep house. And when you do start thinkin about marryin, you keep this in mind. I won't abide you marryin a man that don't go to church. You'll marry an Adventist or nobody."

The Adventist church in Cave Junction was tiny. Just a

few dozen people in the whole thing. No girls my age at all and the only boys was some snot-nose brats that hit me with spitballs. None of them was older'n ten or eleven.

There was some couples with little kids though. Babies. So when I got asked to teach the Cradle Roll class, I was happy to do it. It wasn't really teachin. All I had to do was keep the little ones busy while the service was goin on, and it was a whole lot more interesin than settin through the sermons. Besides, I really liked babies.

Mama and Papa kept sayin I'd be gittin married someday, but I couldn't see how that could happen. There was only one time I even come close to meetin somebody, and Mama run him off.

It was not long before my fourteenth birthday, and the first bright sunny day in months. Papa'd brung a young fella home from town to help clear a place for a garden, and when I went out to take clothes off the line, I seen him. He was leanin on a hoe. Had his shirt off and was lit up in the sun like a gold statue. I never seen anybody so beautiful in my whole life. I stared at him for the longest time before I worked up the nerve to take him a jar of water from the pump.

"Thanks," he said, wipin his hands on his pant legs. "I was real thirsty. I'm Hank, what's your name?" He had the prettiest smile and the bluest eyes and my heart was thumpin so loud I was afraid he could hear it.

"I'm Veda," I said.

Before he even got done drinkin the water, Mama was there tellin me to git myself back in the house. Then she marched over to Papa and I could hear her scoldin him. "Don't you be bringin that trash around here no more," she said, "I don't want his kind takin up with Veda."

She said he was trash, but he wasn't no more trash than we were. I knew that wasn't the real reason anyhow. It was 'cause he wasn't Adventist, and in Mama's opinion, that made us better than him. After that, whenever I went in to town with Papa, I looked for Hank, thinkin he might be at the feed store or where they sold dry goods, but I never did see him. Not even once.

Mama kept me busy. Cleanin, washin clothes, ironin. I worked in the garden, milked our cows, made butter, and learned to bake. But I missed school. Missed talkin to people my own age. The only company we ever got was family and even that didn't happen very much 'cause of how Cave Junction was so far from where the rest of em lived.

My sister Bea's girls, Rheba and Flossie, were younger than me but they knew all sorts of things I didn't know. I didn't like em very much, the way they was always sashayin around in their store-bought dresses, talkin about movie stars. Teasin me. But they was the closest thing I had to girlfriends, and if it wasn't for them I wouldn't of known nothin about nothin.

"Who do you like better?" Flossie asked me one time, holdin up her movie magazine. "Greta Garbo or Jean Harlow?

I shrugged.

"Don't you think Clark Gable is a dreamboat?" Rheba asked.

"I don't know," I said. Her magazine was in her lap, so I couldn't see the picture. "What's he look like?"

They giggled. "Oh Vee, you're such a dope. Don't

you know anything?"

"Shut up," I said. "If you had to live in Cave Junction you wouldn't either." They knew good and well Mama didn't let me go to picture shows or have movie magazines. And they knew I wasn't allowed to listen to anythin but church music. So when Mama couldn't hear us, they taught me some of the new songs. Showed me some of the dances too. I didn't know how they got away with the stuff they got away with. They was Adventist like us, but I guess Bea wasn't as strict as Mama.

It was on one of their visits that they told me I needed to learn how to kiss.

"I don't want to," I said.

"Try it," Rheba said. She balled up her hand and put it on her lips and kind of rubbed it around. "It feels nice. You'll want to when you meet a boy you like. You know how boys are. Always wantin to do things."

"What things?" I asked.

That got em to gigglin again. "You know. Things."

I *didn't* know. How would I? All Mama ever told me about boys was, "Don't let em touch your business."

3

THERE WAS TWO LITTLE GIRLS in the Cradle Roll class that really took to me, so their mother, Mrs. Carlson, asked if I would come work for her. Her husband was a travelin evangelist who was away from home a lot and she said she needed help takin care of the girls. There'd be housework too, so she wanted me to stay at her house all week. Said I could go home and be with my folks over the Sabbath.

"Tell her you'll do it," Mama said. "It'll be good practice for you."

"But don't you need me here?"

"I'll be fine," she said. "You'll be gone soon anyhow. You'll be gittin married and goin off … just like your sisters."

"Why're you so sure I'll even git married?"

"You will, Veda. The Lord will send someone. You'll see."

At first I was real nervous about workin for Mrs. Carlson, but she was patient and I got on real good with the little girls. She give me a real swell room, too. Once the supper dishes was done I could be by myself and do whatever I wanted. I had this stack of old magazines that Flossie had give me, so I was finally able to look at em without Mama knowin. And it was good not to have anybody tell me to stop bitin my nails, or set up straight, or give me things to do 'cause "idle hands is the devil's tools."

One night after I been at the Carlsons' about a year, the missus come in the kitchen where I was peelin potatoes and told me to fix extra. "There's a young man coming to supper," she said. "He'll be staying here at the house." She grinned at me. "He's new in town, so I want you to be nice to him. His name is Raymond Ames. He'll be working with my husband. We told him about you and he wants to meet you. You'll like him."

I knew that had to be Mama's idea. Why else would this Raymond person want to meet me? What was there to tell about me anyway? I wasn't much to look at. I was plain, flat-chested, tall for a girl, and bone-skinny.

As soon as Raymond got there, Mrs. Carlson dragged me into the front room. She hadn't told me he was handsome, but there he was, ever bit as good lookin as Clark Gable. Thick, shiny black hair. A strong, square jaw and eyelashes that had no business bein on a man.

"This is Veda, the girl we told you about," Mrs. Carlson said, pushin me in his direction. "She's a long time member of the church, and she teaches Sabbath School."

He smiled and held out his hand. "How do you do?"

I stood there like a dummy.

When he saw I wasn't goin to shake his hand, he dropped his arm and knelt down in front of the little girls. "I'm Raymond," he said, reachin for the older one. "What's your name?"

"Lydia," she said, twistin back and forth. "I'm four."

Raymond took Anna's tiny hand. "And who are you?" She giggled. "Do you have a name?" Anna grabbed for her mommy. She was only two.

"Tell him your name," Mrs. Carlson said.

Anna giggled again, and Raymond patted her head. "That's all right," he said, "you can tell me later."

I liked how he was with them, and I wished I hadn't acted so dumb.

Mrs. Carlson frowned at me. "Veda, take Raymond's hat. Then come help me get supper on the table."

I put his hat on the rack by the door, and went on in the kitchen.

"Why didn't you say something?" she scolded. "He was anxious to meet you."

Mrs. Carlson put Raymond smack-dab across the table from me so ever time I looked up I seen him lookin at me. I felt like he expected me to say somethin, to join the conversation, but I couldn't think of nothin to say. I felt sick to my stomach and I could barely breathe. Him and Mr. Carlson talked all through supper. About the prayer meetins. The songs Raymond would pick out for the services. The scriptures, the weather, Mr. Carlson's garden, and President Roosevelt.

I liked hearin him talk. Liked his voice. It was slow and sing-songy. And I could tell he was smart 'cause of the all the big words he used. After supper I finished the dishes and started to go to my room, but Mrs. Carlson stopped me. "Why don't you go in the parlor and talk to Raymond?"

"Uh-uh," I said, "I ... I'll just go to my room."

"Oh, go on, he won't bite."

"I can't. I wouldn't know what to say. I don't know ... anythin."

"Just sit with him. Let him do the talking." She give me a little push. "Go on, stop being silly. He's a nice young man. He wants to visit with you."

I crept in, huggin myself to keep from shakin. "Mrs. Carlson said ... she said you want to talk to me?"

Raymond looked up, "Why yes, Veda," he said. He put his finger between the pages of his Bible, to hold his place, and patted the cushion next to him. "Come sit down. Tell me about yourself. How long have you worked here?"

I sat down, edgin as close to the end of the davenport as I could git. "About a year," I said.

"So you must be sixteen? Seventeen? Did you graduate from school?"

"Seventeen," I said. "I didn't graduate. We moved here and Papa..." I hung my head. "I only went to seventh grade."

"Well now," he said, "that's nothing to be ashamed of. I only finished eighth grade myself."

I looked at him. "But..." I said, "you're so smart."

"Well," he said. "I read a lot. The Bible. Newspapers, dictionaries, encyclopedias. And I have a good memory."

I nodded.

"I've just come from Portland," he said, "where I was doing canvass work for the church. Do you know what that means, Veda? To canvass?"

I felt myself blush. "No."

"A canvasser is a person who makes contact with people, in my case, by going door to door, to ask opinions about things, or to inform them of something important."

I pictured the Watkins man with his heavy suitcase full of soaps and such.

"My job was to tell people about the Seventh-day Adventist Church. And to introduce them to Ellen G. White's book, The Great Controversy. Do you know it?"

"My mother has one," I said.

"Have you read it?"

I blushed again. "Some of it."

"Well now, I'll have to get you a copy of your own," he said. "The book describes the end-times. Tells what will happen in the world before Jesus returns."

"Oh," I said. I hoped he would talk about somethin else.

"Canvassing is difficult work," he said. "Most people are close-minded. They won't listen. I've had doors slammed in my face. Dogs sicced on me."

"Why do you do it then?" I asked.

He looked surprised. "It's my calling. I have always wanted to spread God's word, to spread the Adventist truth. Canvassing is a way to take the message to people."

"But if they ain't listnin..."

"God tells us not to be discouraged, Veda. But now Mr. Carlson has given me a chance to do God's work in a different way. I'll be helping with revival meetings."

Raymond talked for a long time. After we said goodnight and I went to my room, I laid awake thinkin about how handsome he was and what a good person he must be to help people git saved. I thought about Mrs. Carlson wantin me to meet him, and Mama sayin the Lord would send me someone to marry. I wondered if Raymond might be the one.

After that first time, we set together pretty regular. He talked and I listened. He told me about his father and mother, about his older brothers and his sister, and the two brothers and a sister that died before he was born. He said his mother was afraid she'd lose him too, 'cause he was sickly, so she kept him out of school for several years and taught him at home. He had always dreamed of bein a minister, wanted to go to the Adventist Academy, but when his mother got sick he had to take care of her and his younger brother. There was never enough money for him to get a formal education.

Most of the time, though, he talked about the Bible. Readin passages to me. Explainin things. One night he was talkin about redemption. "Veda, do you know what that word means?"

"It's gittin yer sins warshed away," I said.

"Waaashed away," he said drawin out the aaahhh. "Having one's sins waaashed away by the power of prayer."

Shamed by how he mocked me, I stood up and started for my room.

"Here, Veda" he said, handin me a piece of paper. "I'd like you to read these."

I took the paper. It was a whole list of Bible verses: 1 Corinthians 1:30, Romans 3:24, Ephesians 1:7, Colossians 1:14. Alone in my room, I looked them up. They all had to do with forgiveness. I wondered what he thought I needed forgiveness for. Mis-pernouncin the word warsh maybe?

When I didn't go to set with him the next night, Mrs. Carlson asked me what was wrong.

"He doesn't like me," I said. "He makes fun of the way I talk."

"Yes he does like you," she said. "He likes you a lot." She told me he hadn't meant to hurt my feelins. "It's just his way. He was trying to help."

So I went back to settin with him. I read what he said to read, and paid attention to how he talked. He knew about all kinds of things, not just the Bible. He could name all the countries, their capitals, and their natural resources. He knew all the mountains and the oceans. Knew the names of flowers and trees. And he told me more about weather than I ever wanted to know. Like what year had the hottest summer and the earliest spring, the last time winter had come this early, and how one year's rainfall compared with all the others. Said he been keepin track since he was a boy. Showed me some of the diaries he wrote it in. It was all there. Ever'day he put in the high and low temperature. If it rained or snowed or the wind blew, and if there was sunshine or fog. Seemed silly to me. I didn't understand why anybody'd go to so much trouble over weather.

"They'd make a lovely couple," I heard Mrs. Carlson tell Mama. "You know, Veda could do worse."

Mama'd already set her sights on Raymond. He was both Adventist and single. When I was home on Sabbath, it was, "that nice young man" this and "that nice young man" that. She repeated what he'd spoke about in church, kept sayin what a good singin voice he had. So, of course, when she heard from Mrs. Carlson that we was keepin company, it put a real spin on her tail. She started askin him to supper pert'near ever week. One Sabbath he stayed so long talkin about the mornin's sermon that Papa got disgusted with him. Kept comin in and sayin things like, "You have a long walk ahead of you, don't you?" and "It's gittin kind of late, don't you think?" Finally Raymond took the hint and said he better be headin back before it got dark.

Mama was real put out at Papa. "Miles," she said, "you oughtn't to have done that, it wasn't polite."

"Well, the boy ought to know when he's wore out his welcome."

"Still, it was rude. He was company."

"I don't see why you're so all fired up over this fella," Papa said. "He can spout the Bible word for word, but he hasn't done a day's work since he's been here. Far as I can tell he don't amount to a good goddamn."

"Miles! Shame on you. He's going to be working with Mr. Carlson, speaking at revivals," Mama said.

"Ha. But can he earn a livin? I know you've got your eye on him for Veda, but I'm tellin you the boy's a fool."

"You hush," Mama said. "He ain't a fool. And Veda needs someone who's a good example to her. Lord knows you ain't. Telling her them stories of yours, teaching her to swear like you done."

"Well," Papa said, "far's I'm concerned a girl needs some spunk. It's better'n bein one a them sourpuss types you're dead set on turnin her into."

"You stay out of it, Miles. That young man likes Veda, and if he does ask her to marry him, I'm goin to be on his side."

Papa might've been right about Raymond's ambition, but he was the first man to give me a second look, and I didn't want him to stop comin around.

22

Raymond stayed at the Carlsons' all winter. He canvassed in Cave Junction when it wasn't rainin too hard, and led the singin at church on Sabbath. And when he wasn't doin things for the church, he chopped wood and cleaned up around the property, cuttin back rose bushes and haulin off piles of dead leaves. The little girls liked him, and he was real good with em, settin with Lydia, who was learnin her letters, readin em stories in that slow, sing-songy way of his.

In early February, Raymond left with Mr. Carlson to do the revival meetins and it wasn't long before Mrs. Carlson started gittin letters. They come from places most people never heard of: Jerome Prairie, O'Brien, Kerbyville, Ruch, Provolt, Merlin. Told about the trouble they was havin gittin around 'cause of all the snow and ice. About havin to meet in cold, dark buildins with no electricity. Havin to use candles and kerosene lamps, and how they built a contraption with a car battery to run their slide projector.

"My husband is so blessed to have the help of that young man," Mrs. Carlson said more than once. And she never mentioned Raymond without addin, "He's going to make a wonderful husband for some lucky girl."

4

March 3, 1937, (Wed.) [Max 67°, Min. 33°.] A chill, dense fog this morning with slight frost; but clear and warm during the day, the warmest of the season so far. I canvassed in and around town today, attending prayer meeting in the evening. Veda went with me to the meeting and on our way back to the Carlson place we became engaged.

IT WAS JUST A ORDINARY prayer meetin, but it was the first time Raymond asked me to go with him. I fixed my hair and put on the new green dress I got when Mrs. Carlson took me with her to Grants Pass. The green brung out the color of my eyes and made me look almost pretty. I had new shoes, too, and I should of known not to wear em since we'd be walkin, but I wanted to look nice.

Raymond talked the whole way, sayin how early spring was this year, pointin out pussy willows and the crocus and daffodils that were comin up in places, sayin how much he liked spring and how much he enjoyed goin on picnics.

"I love picnics too," I said.

He talked about last Sabbath's sermon and what lessons we could learn from it, the film strip he was in charge of settin up at the meetin, and the songs he picked out for us to sing. My feet hurt. I could tell I was goin to have blisters.

When we got to the church I went in the bathroom to look at my feet. There was big watery blisters on both heels and it was all I could do to git my shoes back on. I said a little prayer askin God if, when the meetin was over, He could git somebody to offer us a ride. By the time Raymond got his film wound up and put the projector away, though, ever'body else was gone.

It had got cold and I didn't have a sweater, so when Raymond offered his suit coat, I took it. I tried not to limp, but my feet hurt so bad I wanted to cry. We went for quite a ways with neither one of us sayin anythin, and then Raymond says he wants to ask me a question.

"Go ahead." I hoped he was goin to ask me to go on a picnic.

"Have you accepted Jesus Christ as your personal Lord and Savior?"

Had I accepted Jesus? What kind of question was that? My head buzzed. Afraid I might cry now for sure, I just nodded my head.

"In that case," he said, "will you marry me?"

My jaw dropped. "What did you say?"

"Will you marry me?"

Wasn't there supposed to be somethin between findin out I believed in Jesus Christ and askin me to marry him?

I took off walkin, fast, forgittin my sore feet. My

mouth was dry and I felt like I might be sick. What did I feel about him? He hadn't asked me that. Did he even want to know? Did I know? I had wondered if he might ask me to marry him. Someday. Even hoped he would. But I didn't expect it now. Not yet. He'd never said he liked me. Never said I looked nice. Never held my hand. Nothin.

I could hear him behind me—his breath, his shoes crunchin the gravel—I didn't know what to do. I didn't want to say yes. But I didn't want to say no either. I needed time to think. I wanted to get married, I wanted to have babies. If I told him I needed more time, he might not ask me again. Maybe nobody else would either. I was eighteen years old already. I could end up an old maid.

When I got almost all the way back to the house, I stopped and waited for him. I took a deep breath. "Okay," I said, "I'll marry you."

"Good." He smiled and patted my arm. "That's settled. Let's go in and tell the Carlsons."

"That's wonderful news," Mr. Carlson said, slappin Raymond on the back. Mrs. Carlson hugged me and said she knew the Lord would bring us together. Lydia and Anna hopped up and down like it was a surprise birthday party. Seein how excited they were made me feel better about it too.

"I'm almost twenty-five," Raymond said. "I thought it was time I found a wife."

"Well come on, you two," Mr. Carlson said, "I'll drive you over so you can tell Veda's folks."

I knew Mama'd be tickled to death, but I was nervous about tellin Papa 'cause of what he said about Raymond bein a fool. But Papa didn't say nothin against it. He just set there lookin disappointed the way he did when the Ford had a flat tire. Like he wasn't happy about it but he knew it was bound to happen sooner or later.

Raymond suggested we wait till September to have the weddin, and I thought it was so he could save money to git us a place to live. I said it was okay with me.

"I'll be back from canvassing by then," he said.

"You didn't tell me you were goin away."

"The Lord has called me again."

"But you can't. You need to stay here. So you can find work."

"This is my work, Veda," he laced his fingers together like he was prayin. "Helping people prepare for Christ's return is the only work which can have any effect in bringing about our salvation."

I started to say I meant work that paid money. So we'd have somethin to live on. But he stopped me.

"The Lord provides for his servants, Veda. I'll be back by September. I'll find employment then."

My stomach churned. Papa's "But can he earn a livin?" played over and over inside my head. I knew I wasn't as good a Christian as Raymond. I wasn't even sure I wanted to be. But he'd been helpin folks git ready for Christ's return for a long time and I thought it was time he got himself ready to git married. I didn't really think he'd stay gone that long, though. I thought he'd git tired of havin doors slammed in his face. I thought he'd miss me and come back long before September.

His letters always started "My Dear Veda," or "My Darling," and I'd think he was goin to say he loved me or he missed me, but he didn't. He asked after my health and said he hoped I wasn't workin too hard. Reminded me to read the scriptures. Complained about people not listenin to him, about his feet hurtin from all the walkin. Of course he told me if it was rainin, and how much and for how long. Or if it was hot, he'd tell me if it was normal for this time of year.

Once in a while somebody'd give him a ride back to Cave Junction and he'd spend Sabbath with my folks and me. He looked a little worse off ever'time. Clothes all wrinkled and dusty, shoes wore down. I always wondered if the Lord really was takin care of Raymond's needs. Seemed to me, he could use a haircut and a decent pair of shoes.

5

EVER'TIME I SEEN MY NIECE FLOSSIE, she had a new boyfriend. She'd say things like, "He's all over me... He begs me to sleep with him... He's crazy for me... Says we'll git married as soon as his ship comes in but he loves me too much to wait." It was always the same story. But always a new guy. "That last sonofabitch was two-timin me," she'd say. "I seen him with somebody else. You're so lucky to have Raymond."

I wondered if she meant it. She always made fun of how proper Raymond was, called him a stick in the mud. And I wondered if I really was lucky. I mean it was true I never had to worry about him takin up with some floozy, but I felt sort of jealous of Flossie. I wished Raymond would say he was crazy for me and couldn't stand to wait. I wished he would kiss me and beg me. I wished he would at least touch me.

"Why won't he even say he loves me?" I whined to Mama. "Why can't he be romantic?"

"Romance is a bunch of foolishness," she said. "It's what gets girls in trouble. They'll promise the moon, some of em. Look at Flossie. Thank God you have a wonderful Christian man like Raymond."

"I know, Mama, but I want him to be in love. *I* want to be in love. And I don't even know what that's supposed to feel like."

All she said to that was, "Once you're married you'll know."

Romance. I thought about it all the time. Dreamed about it. Studied pictures in magazines. Happy couples holdin hands, laughin, or just lookin at each other. You could tell they was in love. It was how I wanted Raymond to look at me.

"That's not real life," Mama said. "It's all put on. Throw them magazines away. You're just settin yourself up for disappointment."

In my letters to Raymond, I called him Sweetheart. I said I loved him and missed him and couldn't wait for him to come back. I kept hopin he would write the same things to me, but he didn't seem to catch on. His next letter would come and it'd have the weather report, say how nobody would buy the books he was sellin, complain about religious prejudice. And folded inside the same envelope, corrected with red pencil like schoolwork, would be my last letter to him.

In June, Mrs. Carlson told me she wouldn't need me anymore. "My girls are old enough to help around the house," she said, "and you need to be with your mother so she can prepare you for marriage."

I had some money saved up for a weddin dress and it took me weeks to decide on the right one. It was in the Monkey Ward catalog. White organdy with a long skirt gathered at the waist. It had a sweetheart neckline and long fitted sleeves. It was perfect. I sent off my order and couldn't wait for it to come. Then I sent in one more order. For a pair of good black oxfords for Raymond, size nine and a half.

I spent a lot of dreamtime with that catalog, runnin my fingers over the pages of pretty things: China dishes, silverware, table linens, shiny pots and pans. Things I knew we couldn't afford. Mama said to forgit about havin new. She went through her things and give me what she thought I needed.

"Food tastes the same no matter what it's ate off of. You're just startin out. You and Raymond can buy nicer things later on."

It was a cold spring that year and the garden got a late start. Except for the peas and lettuce, nothin was up, so there wasn't a whole lot to do. Mama was makin me a patchwork quilt, so I set with her and helped her stitch. We'd turn on the radio and listen to her favorite programs and the news. It was durin that time when Amelia Earhart turned up missin. Nobody knew what happened to her. For days and days it was almost the only thing people talked about. The people on the radio, me and my folks, people at church. We was all prayin for her, and when they finally give up searchin, I was heartbroke. I wrote to Raymond about it, but he didn't have nothin to say. That was another thing that bothered me about him, how he didn't care about things like that.

With him away, my feelins were all over the place. I went back and forth in my mind about marryin him. I made up speeches in my head. *I think you're a wonderful person, but I can't marry you. 'Cause … you don't really love me… You don't care about anythin but church… I'd git in your way… I'd just hold you back.* Or I might say, *Please don't hate me for sayin this, but I think I'm supposed to feel somethin and I don't.*

Then he'd come back for a Sabbath and I seen it different. Settin next to him in church, with people fawnin over him, I felt special 'cause he was special. I seen how kind he was. How good. How faithful. And marryin him seemed right after all. Besides, it was too late to change my mind. The weddin was all planned. I had my clothes and my dishes and kettles all boxed up and Raymond's shoes had come in the mail. The only thing I was still waitin on was my dress.

I told myself it would turn out fine. If I didn't love him now, if he didn't love me, it would change once we got married. That's what Mama said, "Love deepens once you're married." We would be happy together. We'd have beautiful babies, and he'd be a wonderful father. I wanted to throw my arms around him and kiss him real hard. I wanted to see what it felt like. See if he kissed me back. But I was too bashful to do it.

And when he went away again, I went back to worryin. He said he would return before September, but he didn't say how long before. July went by and we got into August. I knew he still didn't have a job lined up and I didn't know what kind of work he would look for. He couldn't git paid for preachin without bein ordained. He had experience goin door to door for the church, but could he sell Watkins products or vacuum cleaners? He was good with words and numbers, so maybe he could git some kind of office job.

It was a week before the weddin, and Flossie and Rheba was with me in my bedroom. I was showin em my "tru-so." That was the fancy name for my new underpants and brassieres and the pretty white nightgown Mama got for me. Flossie was puttin on lipstick, and Rheba was admirin herself in the mirror on my dresser. She kept turnin this way and that, smoothin her skirt down over her hips.

"What do you think?" she asked.

"It's nice," I told her. "I sure hope my dress gits here on time."

"Are you scared?"

"About the dress? Kind of. It's been almost three months since I ordered it."

"No, not that. Are you scared about … you know, the wedding night?"

"A little."

"Do you know what he'll do? How he'll do it?"

"Not really."

"We'll tell you if you want us to," Flossie chimed in. She was in the middle of puttin on lipstick, her top lip was bright red.

"No, I don't want you to," I said. "You and Rheba already told me things. How do I know you're not makin it up? You never been married."

"How are you going to find out then? Somebody's got to tell you."

"I'm goin to go talk to Bea. She's been married a long time. You and Rheba stay here. And you better not let Mama see you with that lipstick on."

My sister Bea was by herself on the back porch with a pile of string beans in her lap. I set down across from her and picked up a handful.

"Bea," I said, snappin the end off one and pullin the string down its side, "I'm worried about … you know … the weddin night. Do you think Raymond knows what to do?"

"Oh sure, honey. He has two older brothers. They've told him I'm sure." Then she started explainin things. About his body and my body and what went where and ... she called it mar-i-tal relations.

"Will it hurt?"

"A little, the first time. But after that, it'll be nice, you'll see."

"I worry about Raymond," I said. "He's so serious all the time. He's never even said he loves me. Was Gabe like that before you got married?"

"Well, no. But Raymond's the quiet type. He'll be all right. Once you have marital relations, he'll loosen up."

6

September 26, 1937 (Sunday) [Max 86°, Min. 36°.] Clear but unseasonably hot and oppressive with smoke and haze on the horizon. There are ongoing forest fires in many places around southern Oregon. It's the fifth sharp, cool morning in a row. Our wedding day! Witnessed by my family from Salem and many other friends and relatives, Veda and I were united in marriage by Elder Swensen at our little church in Cave Junction this evening.

WHEN THE PRETTY ORGANDY DRESS from the catalog come, too late to send it back, it wasn't white like in the picture. It was yellow. Yellow! I might as well wear a big sign sayin I'm not a virgin. I cried for two days.

I was still upset on the day of the weddin, and Mama scolded me, told me to straighten myself up. She said nobody would notice the color.

Old Mrs. Haney set at the piano and plunked out "Here Comes the Bride" while Papa led me to the front of the church. My ears burned the whole way. I could hear folks whisperin, and I knew they was sayin a

Adventist girl should be wearin a white weddin dress, sayin I must not be a good girl after all. I snuck a sideways glance at Raymond to see if he noticed I wasn't wearin white, but he wasn't even lookin at me. He was standin there with his head bowed, lookin respectable. His suit was pressed, he had a haircut, and he had on his new shoes.

I looked down at the yellow mums I was holdin, and felt even worse. I'd had my heart set on white roses with pink ribbons like a bouquet I seen in a magazine, but Mama said it was foolishness to pay money when we had all them flowers out back.

I stared hard at the dandruff on Elder Swensen's dark suit, and tried to hold back tears while he read some words about a wife cleavin to her husband. He asked Raymond to repeat after him, promisin to love, honor, and keep me. When it was my turn, he changed the words to love, honor, and obey. Then he told Raymond to take my hand, and we got down on our knees for a prayer. It was the first time Raymond had held my hand, and I started to think about his hands on my body. My face got hot and I could hear my heart. When the minister said, "You may kiss the bride," Raymond leaned over and give me a quick kiss on the mouth. The sweetish tang of his breath surprised me.

Afterwards people kept slappin Raymond on the back, sayin congratulations, and tellin me how lucky I was. Then soon as we got off by ourselves, Raymond said he had to leave in the mornin for a job. It was in Salem, he said, and he didn't know how long he'd be gone.

"I thought we were gittin our own place," I said.

"We will. Just as soon as I get back."

"But what about tonight? Where'll we stay?"

"With your folks, I expect. I have to leave early."

So that was it? I knew I should be glad he had a job, but I wanted things to start out different. I wanted us to be alone. I wanted him to take me someplace. All these months I'd wondered what our weddin night would be like, and now it wasn't even goin to happen.

The supper in Mama's kitchen was as plain as the weddin. Potatoes, fried eggplant, string beans, and them breaded tomatoes that always made me gag. There was a cake, but it didn't even have a bride and groom on top to make it special. Papa kept tryin to start a conversation with Raymond's dad, but it wasn't goin nowhere, and Raymond's mother picked at her food like she was used to better. Then Mama went and told Raymond's folks they could have my bed, that me and Raymond would sleep in the front room.

Raymond said he'd be fine on the davenport, and Papa set up a cot for me. I put on my pretty new nightgown, but Raymond didn't notice it. Just said for me to kneel down with him so we could pray. While he was busy thankin God for givin him a "good wife to be his helpmate," I prayed that Raymond would turn out to be a good husband, that he would learn to love me.

"Goodnight, dear," he said, kissin me on the cheek. He got into his bed and I got into mine. It was pitch dark and it felt strange havin him so close. I could hear him punchin at his pillow, rustlin against the sofa fabric, gruntin and clearin his throat. I wanted him to come over to me, to touch me, but I didn't know how to tell him.

I didn't go to sleep for a long time. I listened to the house groan and creak, to the trees sweep against the windows, and the embers pop in the woodstove. All kinds of things run through my mind. I wondered when he'd be back from his job. I wondered where we'd live and what our life was goin to be like. And I wondered how many other disappointments I had ahead of me.

7

November 3, 1937 (Wed.) [Max. 60°, Min. 38.] Foggy and chilly all the a.m. but clearing and mild and pleasant in the p.m. Veda arrived today and began to get things settled and unpacked and the place cleaned up. I was in bed with a bad cold all morning.

I'D BEEN MARRIED FOR ALMOST six weeks and I was still a virgin. When I went to church people slid their eyes over me the way folks do to see if I was walkin different. I hadn't seen Raymond since the weddin, I was still sleepin at Mama's house, and still worryin about what sex would feel like.

When Raymond got back to Grants Pass, he called Papa and asked him to drive me there. He'd got us a place in a shabby two-story roomin house with six mailboxes nailed up by the front door. Number four had Raymond's name on it. He was in his room, in bed, with a hot water bottle and a pile of blankets. The room was cold and it smelled like Vicks VapoRub. A cast-iron stove stood in the corner, but the fire had gone out.

I started to fuss over Raymond, but he told me not to come too close. He didn't want to "communicate" his cold to me. I left my coat on and got a fire goin in the stove. Then while I waited for the room to git warm, I checked to see if there was any food in the cupboards. All he had was half a jar of peanut butter and some Postum. Luckily I'd brung a few groceries with me, so I fixed some soup hopin it would make him feel better.

He was sick for a whole week, and by the time he come out of it and told me he felt better, I had my period. I was nervous and couldn't think of how to tell him. I puttered around, doin some wash, cookin a meal. Raymond spent the day readin his Bible and writin in one of his journals. When we set down to eat supper, he started tellin me some of what the Bible says about a good wife. She should be modest. Be sober and unworldly. Be careful what she wears and what she says. He went on and on, and by the time he finished, I was really scared. I knew that tellin him about my period wouldn't be modest, and as it got closer to bedtime, I started to panic.

I put on my nightgown and took extra time washin my face. Raymond got down on his knees by the bed and waited for me to come and say prayers. There was a wood floor under my bare feet, but it could of been hot coals for all I knew. The only thing I could feel was that wad of Kotex between my legs.

I went and crouched down next to him. "Our Heavenly Father," he said, "we ask your blessing as we come together for the first time as man and wife..."

Oh, God, I thought, *not tonight. Please. Please, let him change his mind.* I was afraid I said it out loud, but Raymond's eyes was still closed, he was still prayin.

"...keep us under your protection and give us the strength and courage we need to perform our duty to you. In Jesus name, amen."

Raymond got in the bed and pulled the blankets back for me. I slid in real slow, throat dry and heart poundin like a war drum. I stayed close to the edge, but he reached over and started pullin up my nightgown. When he felt it, he jumped like he touched a hot stove.

"What is that?"

"Uh ... a ... a pad ... I'm havin my period."

It was dark in the room. I felt him yank the blankets. The bed heaved and I heard him cross the floor. "You should have told me, Veda," he said. "You should have told me."

"I ... I wanted to but ... I," I stammered. "Why? Is it bad?"

"Leviticus, Veda. Leviticus 15:19-20: 'And if a woman have an issue, and her issue in her flesh be blood, she shall be put apart seven days: and whosoever toucheth her shall be unclean until the even. And every thing that she lieth upon in her separation shall be unclean: every thing also that she sitteth upon shall be unclean...' " I could hear him arrangin his blanket. "I will sleep on the sofa until this business is over."

"I'm sorry," I blubbered, "I wanted to tell you ... I didn't know how..." I laid there ashamed and hurt and sick to my stomach, wantin my mother, wantin to go home. Somebody should of told me this would happen. Somebody should of told me about Leviticus.

Raymond didn't mention it in the mornin and neither did I. A whole week went by before he tried again, askin first if I was "well." We said prayers and got into the bed. I was tight as a bowstring, not knowin what his first move would be.

"Dear?" It sounded like a question.

"Mmm-mm," I mumbled back.

I felt the bedsprings give and he was on me, pushin my legs apart with his knee. He kissed me, and then all of a sudden he was pressin against me, hard, and I … it hurt somethin awful. He lifted his weight off me and pushed into me again, and again. His breath was fast and heavy. Then he rolled off.

"You okay?"

I laid there burnin and raw, wonderin if it was supposed to hurt this much. He didn't say nothin else, and pretty soon I could tell by his breathin he was asleep.

I was sore in the mornin and there was blood in my underpants. I didn't know if that was supposed to happen or if it meant somethin was wrong. Bea hadn't told me about that either.

I was all tensed up the next time, expectin to feel the same raw soreness, but it didn't hurt near as much. There was a few minutes of him bouncin up and down, and then it was over. I wanted to like it, and I tried to. I kept on hopin to feel somethin, like Bea said, somethin nice.

8

November 30, 1937 (Tues.) [Max. 45°, Min. 32°.] Slight frost with cold fog this morning which lasted all day. Extremely chilly and disagreeable. In contrast to last year, this November was one of the rainiest on record here with 10.15 inches of rain. We finished the bulbs and got our pay this evening. I have another bad cold.

MARRIAGE WASN'T TURNIN OUT to be like I imagined. Raymond was kind, always askin after my health, tellin me not to overdo, but he was still serious as a Sabbath sermon. He hadn't loosened up at all.

When he had work around Grants Pass, he set out before daylight, walkin, and it was well after dark when he got back. If the job was farther away, he took the Greyhound bus and stayed in a cheap hotel. I was lonesome. My folks was clear out at Cave Junction and I didn't have a way to git there. I missed my Papa's funny stories, I missed Mama, I even missed seein Flossie and Rheba. I wanted company. I wanted to laugh.

When Raymond was home, he was sober and grown up all the time. He treated me like a student, tellin me what I could do, what I should read, givin me Bible verses to memorize. I told myself I was lucky to have a good husband, that I shouldn't think about what I didn't have, but I couldn't help it. I wanted to git out of the apartment, go someplace, but it was cold and the rain turned the roads to mud. So except for when I needed to buy food, I stayed inside. And when I couldn't take any more of what Raymond told me to read, I got out my old magazines and leafed through em. I done it so many times they was fallin apart, but I didn't dare spend money on new ones.

"Couldn't we git a radio?" I asked Raymond one of the times he was home.

He said no. "It will put ideas in your head. Worldly ideas."

I told him Mama had a radio, and she always had it tuned to The Voice of Prophesy. "I could learn a lot from The Voice of Prophesy."

He still said no. "You'd be tempted to listen to other things. Lead us not into temptation, Veda. Remember that. You mustn't let yourself be led astray."

Raymond was right. I would have listened to other things. Other kinds of music. Popular songs like the ones Rheba and Flossie taught me. Songs like "Puttin on the Ritz" and "Good Night Irene."

Once winter came on, Raymond, like thousands of others, had almost no work. I fretted about how we would buy groceries and pay our rent, but he told me not to worry, that the Lord would provide for us. He reminded me how people from church often times asked us to supper. Reminded me of the box of hand-me-downs Mrs. Shaunessy sent over.

Her dead husband's suit was too good to throw away, she said, and there was some shoes and a couple of dresses she thought I could use. Raymond put the suit on. It made him look like a undertaker, but it fit him perfect.

"Try the dresses on," he said.

"I don't want to. They'll make me look like an old woman."

"Veda, we can't turn down perfectly good clothes."

So just to show him, I put one on and stuffed the front to make it look like my breasts were down around my waist like Mrs. Shaunessy's. Then I put on the pair of lace-up oxfords, scrunched my stockins around my ankles, and groaned a little about my "rhumatiz" for effect. Instead of thinkin it was funny, Raymond bawled me out. Said I ought to be ashamed, makin fun of a good Christian lady like that.

It made me mad, him always bein such a sorehead, and I decided to teach him a lesson. The next day I got my scissors and cut every other stitch in the crotch of the dead man's suit pants. Sabbath mornin, when we set down in the front pew of the church, I heard the seam give way. Raymond's eyes got round as saucers, and it was all I could do to keep a straight face.

"Now Brother Ames will lead us in a hymn," the pastor said, and Raymond shook his head. Then the pastor asked him again, "Will you lead us in a song, Brother Ames?" Raymond shook his head harder.

"Well," the pastor said, "it appears Brother Ames isn't feeling well."

After the closin prayer, folks kept comin up to us sayin they hoped Raymond felt better soon. He nodded but he didn't budge, just set there with his nose in his Bible, like he was studyin it. After ever'body left, he got up and hightailed it home faster'n I ever seen him walk, holdin his hat behind him the whole way. I didn't even try to keep up. I didn't want him to see me laughin.

I was disappointed in Raymond, and I knew he was disappointed in me. He had picked me to marry 'cause I wasn't "silly like other young women," and here I was cuttin up when I was supposed to be serious. I wanted to be a good wife, and I tried. I really did. I studied the Bible with him in the evenins, and prayed with him, and read the lessons he told me to read. I fixed our meals and kept our place clean. Washed and mended his clothes, shined his Sabbath shoes, and made sure I had all my chores done before sundown on Friday so I wouldn't be doin any work on the Lord's Day. I even double stitched the seam in his trousers. But it still bothered me somethin awful that I couldn't make him laugh.

December was a miserable month. Cold and rainy, lots of fog. Raymond went out day after day, lookin for work. But if somebody said to come on Saturday, he turned em down. He got a few little piddly jobs. Pruned a few bushes. Cleaned up a yard or two. And he was always comin down with colds from bein out in the weather.

When I learned about the program called Works Progress Administration, I tried to git Raymond to sign up. He wouldn't do it. Said he'd worked on crews like that in Salem once and wouldn't do it again. Said it was all riff-raff workin them jobs, men that smoked tobacco and used crude language, and he couldn't abide bein around people like that. By January we didn't have rent money and I had to ask my folks to take us in.

"On one condition," Papa said. "Raymond signs up with the WPA."

Raymond said he couldn't.

"Looky here," Papa said, "you married my daughter and you promised to take care of her. If you don't come up with a better idea, I'm goin to drag you down to that office and sign you up myself."

Raymond set in a corner the whole evenin, slump-shouldered, knees together, poutin. I didn't like Papa talkin to my husband that way, but I didn't think Raymond should be turnin down work either. Finally, after a week of not findin anythin, he give in and let Papa drive him to the government office. He was issued a card and told to come back the next day ready to spend a week workin in the woods. Papa was pleased, but then when he seen Raymond gittin his kit ready, he got provoked all over again.

"That boy don't have sense enough to make up his own bedroll," he told Mama. She always took Raymond's side against Papa, but I think even she was beginnin to wonder if Raymond would ever amount to a hill of beans.

9

January 18, 1938 (Tues.) [Max. 55°, Min 44°.] A delightfully soft, mild, springlike day; changeable and unsettled with light showers. I left Veda's folks' place to go to work for the WPA.

RAYMOND GOT TWO, sometimes three days' work a week, and always come back complainin about the other men and their filthy habits. In March he got laid off, and not wantin to deal with Papa again, bought bus tickets to Salem. We could stay with his folks, he said, and find work there. "You will like it," he said, "Salem is pretty this time of year."

I was lookin forward to seein Salem and the pretty new Capitol buildin Raymond told me about, but I was nervous about his family. His sister and younger brother still lived at home, and I didn't want us to be in the way. Besides, I had only met his parents, and that was just the one time, at the weddin, and I didn't think his mother liked me.

It was late afternoon when we got off the bus. Raymond said it was just a short walk to his folks' house, so I picked up my suitcase and followed him, gawkin at the big houses with their pretty green lawns and flowerin trees. The tulips and daffodils. After ten or twelve blocks, though, things started lookin shabby. Rundown places with plain dirt yards. Ragged little kids and sad-eyed men set on porches starin at us. My arms started to ache and my stomach growled. "Is your ma expectin us for supper?" I asked. "I hope they haven't already ate."

"Eaten," Raymond said, "I hope they haven't already *eaten*."

"Well anyhow," I said, wishin I had the nerve to kick him, "I'm hungry."

Their house was way back off the road. It had a sorry lookin porch and needed a coat of paint, but it did have a big vegetable garden off to one side.

Raymond's mother, Myrtle, come runnin out, carryin on like Raymond was Jesus Christ himself. I almost expected her to bring a dishpan and wash his feet right there in front of me. She give me a quick once over, nodded, and herded us into the kitchen where the whole family was waitin.

There was Raymond's two older brothers, Al and Norman, their wives and little boys, his sister Helena, and the youngest brother, Everett, who looked enough like Raymond to be his twin. After I been told all their names, we set down to the table and they started askin Raymond questions, tellin him what work they been doin, and what jobs he might be able to git. I set there feelin awkward, watchin em talk and eat. Nobody said nothin to me. It was like I wasn't there at all. I looked over at Nathaniel, Raymond's dad. He winked at me and I smiled back. I decided he was probably the only one in the family that might become my friend.

When supper was over, Myrtle showed us to Helena's room. "You can have her bed while you're here," she said.

"I don't want to put her out..." I stammered. "Maybe we should — "

"Helena will be fine on the sofa," Myrtle said lookin at Helena. "She doesn't mind, do you dear?"

Helena shot me a look hot enough to melt paint. Once I got a good look at the bed, though, I figured she got the better deal. It sagged so deep in the middle I was afraid once we got in it we wouldn't be able to git back out.

Watchin Myrtle and Raymond together grated on my nerves. The two of em spent most of their time huddled in a corner readin to each other while I cooked and washed dishes. Raymond's dad never said much, but ever once in a while he'd look at me and wink. I got the feelin he knew what I was up against.

Helena's bed wasn't just lumpy, it was loud. If we moved at all, the springs squealed like a train comin to a halt, so Raymond barely touched me. The whole three and a half weeks we were there Raymond didn't find any work and I was itchin to leave. I was tired of the way his mother doted on him, and I was afraid she'd have him back in short pants if we stayed any longer.

We went back to my folks' place and Raymond got work in a pear orchard. After a couple weeks he was able to rent us a little walk-up flat in Grants Pass. Alone in our own place, I thought things would be better. I thought Raymond would act more like a husband. I teased him and tried to git him to cuddle, but he would squirm away. In our early months together he'd quoted from the apostle Paul to the Corinthians, "The husband should fulfill his marital duty to his wife, and likewise the wife to her husband." It seemed that was all sex was to him, a duty. Once in a while he'd strip down to his union suit, say his prayers, turn out the lights, and climb on top of me. I wanted more than that. I wanted the lights on. I wanted him to look at me, see me with my clothes off. I wanted to see him. But I couldn't tell him that. Wantin those things … desirin … deep down I felt it must be sinful.

10

June 23, 1938, (Thur.) [Max 93°, Min 51°.]   Another brilliantly clear, glorious day at the peak of the year but very hot and very dry with extremely critical forest fire conditions prevailing. Veda was sick again this morning with stomach trouble.

IT WAS TERRIBLE HOT all week. At first I thought it was the weather makin me feel sick. Either that or it was the same stomach trouble Raymond had. When it didn't pass, I told Mama. She took ahold of my face and turned it up so she could look in my eyes, "Honey, don't you know what this is? You're goin to have a baby. I'm sure of it."

I was so worried about rent money and how we were goin to buy groceries with Raymond not workin much, I forgot to notice I wasn't gittin my period. But once it sunk in, what Mama said, I got excited. A baby would change ever'thin. Once Raymond knew he was goin to be a father he'd look for a different kind of work. Somethin steady. I couldn't wait to tell him.

He seemed pleased. Not excited, but pleased. Told

me not to worry. He'd find work. He kept askin around for day labor jobs, pickin fruit, hops, whatever was in season. Sometimes people we knew hired him to do yard work or chop firewood, but we barely got by. I got over my mornin sickness and, except for the money worries, I felt good. My pregnancy was startin to show.

"You should stay home from church," Raymond said to me one mornin.

"Why would I do that?" I had on one of the maternity smocks my sister Zelda had give me and I thought I looked nice.

"You've been feelin poorly."

"Not anymore. I feel fine now."

"Well, I just thought since…"

"You're embarrassed," I teased. "You don't want people to see I'm pregnant. You are happy about the baby, aren't you?"

"Of course I am. It's just that —"

"Well I'm goin with you," I said.

For the first time in my life I felt pretty. My color was good, and I finally had breasts. The bigger I got, the more uncomfortable Raymond seemed. I think my pregnancy bothered him the way my periods did. He didn't want to be around it. When the baby started to kick, I tried to git him to put his hand on my belly, but he pulled away, said he didn't care for that sort of thing.

11

February 3, 1939 (Fri.) [Max 48°, Min 33°.] Cold rain mixed with snow but warming up considerably during the day with a light snowstorm. I went back to work on the WPA today. Our little Rosalie was born at 1:05 a.m. at the maternity home.

WHEN MY LABOR PAINS started Raymond froze up like a cornstalk in winter. Stood there wringin his hands and didn't have the faintest idea what to do.

"Go call my brother," I said. "He'll drive us to the maternity home." Raymond didn't move. "Listen to me!" I said louder. "Go next door and use their telephone. Call Laird."

He was only gone a couple of minutes, and when he come back our neighbor lady Mrs. Hancock was with him. She asked me how far apart my pains were and told me to "pant like a dog" when they came. Then she told Raymond to make himself useful and go get my suitcase.

When Laird showed up, him and Raymond helped me git in the car. All the way to the maternity home

Raymond set bent over, grippin his stomach like he was the one havin labor pains. The nurse at the front desk told him he was havin a case of nerves. She left him in the waitin room and took me to a ward where another nurse helped me take off my clothes. The pains were comin real close together and I was scared.

"You'll be fine, dearie," she said, "it'll be better once you're settled."

She put me on a bed with a rubber sheet on it and brought in a bowl of warm water. She washed my breasts and stomach and all down between my legs. Then she started shavin me down there.

"Don't," I said, but she went on ahead, sayin it had to be done.

The pains kept comin, harder and harder, and by the time she was done, I was hurtin so bad she could of shaved my whole head, too, and I wouldn't of cared.

When I was "settled," she brought Raymond in to see me. He looked so sickly, she told him he wasn't no use to me and maybe he should just go on home. He took her at her word and left. He probably wouldn't of been no help, but I didn't think he had any business leavin. He was the one got me pregnant and he could at least stay and see how much it hurt.

The pains went on past midnight. I was hollerin and sweatin, and they give me some kind of gas to breathe that made me feel woozy and the doctor was sayin to push. Then I heard him say, "It's a girl," and I started to cry. They brought her over and laid her on my chest, and all of a sudden I felt happier than I ever had before in my whole life. She was my very own baby. Mine. Ever bit of that hurtin was worth it. I looked at her, all sticky and smeared up, and I knew I would die before I ever let anythin bad happen to her.

That afternoon Raymond come in all smiles, sayin he wanted to name her Myrtle after his mother but I told him no. I said I didn't like it and she wouldn't either. Besides I already had a name picked out. Rosalie. I wanted her name to be Rosalie.

It was nice in the maternity home. The nurses all so cheerful, bringin Rosalie right to my bed, showin me how to change her diaper and clean around her navel. Teachin me how to git her tiny mouth over the whole brown part of my nipple.

They brought her to me every four hours and I held her to my breast. I watched her little cheeks go in and out, uncurled her tiny fingers, and unwrapped the blanket to look at ever single part of her. On the third day, I felt my milk come in. There was a sharp pain and then this warm feelin spread all through me. That's when I knew I was meant to be a mother, that havin babies was what God put me on this earth to do.

As the days went by I got more sure of myself. I loved holdin my baby, watchin her eyes flutter, seein her squint up at me. As soon as she started to fuss, my milk would start. Just like that. I couldn't git over how my body knew what to do. I loved watchin her nurse, loved how her little hands kneaded my breasts. It seemed strange, but the way I felt nursin my baby was how I thought lovemakin would be. Who would of guessed I had to have a baby to find out how that felt.

I was there for ten days, bein waited on and gittin to know my baby. Mama, my sisters, people from the church, even the pastor come to visit. I walked em to the nursery window and showed em that of all the babies, mine was prettiest.

We were livin in a flat on F Street that cost twelve

dollars a month. It was damp and cold and the landlady refused to turn the heat up. I wore sweaters over my sweaters and wrapped Rosalie in layers of blankets. Raymond got back on with the WPA and was gittin a few days' work here and there, most of it around Grants Pass, so he was home nights and I wasn't lonesome anymore. I was thrilled with my baby. I could set for hours doin nothin but watchin her tiny face change, one second all screwed up in a frown, and then all peaceful. I told Mama she was already startin to smile at me. Mama said it was just gas. I knew better.

Rosalie had her daddy's eyes and dark hair, and while Raymond was happy to take credit for her good looks, he never held her. He acted almost afraid. I didn't mind all that much, him lettin her alone, 'cause I was happy not havin to share her. I told myself it'd be different when she was bigger. When he could read to her and teach her things. He would like that.

Raymond spent his evenins studyin the Bible and copyin down scripture. And ever night before goin to bed, he wrote in his diary. Sometimes I looked at what he wrote. There was always the high temperature and the low temperature. How this day's weather compared to other years. Sometimes he mentioned a job he was on, or a meetin he went to at church, but except for way back, when he put in about our engagement and the weddin, and then sayin our baby was born, there was nothin in there about us at all.

12

February 14, 1940 (Wed.) [Max 47°, Min. 36°.] Some rain falling last night, but cloudy, cool and damp today. We've had 5.07 inches of rain this month and 10.51 inches since Jan 1. The project I've been on is finished and I have been laid off from the WPA again. We are going to move in with Mrs. Oliver, a woman we know from our church.

I WASN'T HAPPY ABOUT sharin a house, but we were about to be kicked out of where we were livin and I didn't have a better idea. Mrs. Oliver wasn't bein charitable. She needed the extra income. We kept to ourselves, but whenever I was in the kitchen she spied on me to make sure I didn't use her groceries, or didn't run up the electric bill by turnin on a extra light bulb. She treated me like I didn't have good sense. Told me a hundred times to mind I didn't burn the house down.

When Raymond didn't have work he hung around writin in his books instead of goin out lookin for a job, and it was gittin on my nerves. One of my brother-in-law's friends who had got on with the Post Office said they was givin the Civil Service test down at the courthouse. "Tell Raymond to go down and apply," Gabe said. "He would be real good at that kind of work, the way he likes numbers and record keeping and all."

I tried my damnedest, but Raymond wouldn't go. He had it in his head it would mean workin Saturdays. Wouldn't even go find out if it was true or not. The Bible did say to rest on the Sabbath, but it seemed to me if God give a man a family, He'd want him to take care of em. Ever'time Gabe asked me about it, I had to tell him Raymond hadn't gone. It wasn't the first time I was disappointed in Raymond, but it was the first time I felt ashamed.

I was pregnant again, Raymond had no work, and ever'body was talkin about America gittin into the war over in Europe. The whole idea had Raymond scared to death. Even if our pastor vouched for his religious convictions, he knew he could still git drafted. He could have to go and be a medic or somethin. So instead of usin his time to look for work, he went up in the mountains and prayed to be spared from military service. "For the sake of his dear little family."

August 16, 1940 (Fri.)[Max 92°, Min 52°.] Becoming sweltering hot today beginning another heat wave although very cool in morning, The temperature went up to 92°, the warmest since Sunday. Veda went to the Maternity home this evening to await the arrival of our little one.

I spent all day Friday cannin peaches, workin fast as I could to git done before Raymond got home. Once the sun went down, it'd be the Sabbath, and if I wasn't done by then, he'd be mad. I was sticky and hot, and Rosalie was cranky. She kept grabbin my skirt, whinin, wantin to be picked up. It was nerve wrackin havin her underfoot with all the kettles of boilin water around, and I was worried about her. And havin to reach clear out over my big belly to lift the pots off the stove was killin my back.

Mrs. Oliver wasn't doin a thing except stickin her nose in ever few minutes to see if I was done yet, and I was itchin to say it wouldn't hurt her to pick Rosalie up and keep her out of my way. Or tell her if she helped me out she could have her damn kitchen back a whole lot sooner. But I already been got after too many times by Raymond for speakin my mind.

What I wanted to do was set down and put my feet up, but I still had to fix somethin for supper. I looked in our cupboard and decided Raymond'd have to be satisfied with oatmeal. Oatmeal with some of these here peaches.

I was takin the last ten quarts from the kettle when I felt a gush of water. Raymond come in the back door and seen me standin in a puddle, with peach juice runnin down my arms and a screamin toddler wrapped around my legs.

"My water broke," I told him. "Sabbath or no Sabbath, I'm in labor and there ain't no stoppin it."

Robert Raymond came into the world squallin his head off and he didn't stop for three solid months. Rosalie was such a easy baby, but Bobby was altogether different. When I tried to nurse him he drew up his little legs and screamed bloody murder. I walked the floor with him till I was dead on my feet, and Raymond never once offered to take him. When the cryin got on his nerves, he went out and left me to deal with a screamin baby and a eighteen-month-old that wanted attention.

The doctor said my milk was givin the baby gas pains and I should put him on store-bought formula. A week's worth cost almost as much as groceries for the rest of us and Raymond didn't think I should. But he wasn't the one sufferin the colic. Or the cryin either. So I bought the formula and cut back on what I ate. I didn't have much of a appetite anyhow.

Soon as I started givin Bobby canned formula, he stopped screamin and turned into a sweet-natured little guy. Slept sometimes four hours before he woke up needin to be fed again. Mrs. Oliver stopped complainin about him, and I started to feel more kindly toward her. It couldn't of been easy puttin up with our squallin baby all them months.

Rosalie talked early, pickin up words almost as soon as she heard em, and Raymond started takin more interest in her. Teachin her to sing songs like "Jesus Loves Me" and "This Little Light of Mine," and gittin a kick out of showin her off. Her tries at "Bobby" come out "Bubby," and Raymond picked it up. Pretty soon we were all callin him Bubby.

But then both the kids come down with the croup, and Mrs. Oliver got all hateful again. Treated us like lepers. Went so far as to mark off a part of the kitchen to make sure none of our things touched hers. I was worried sick about the kids, and so was Raymond. We both set up nights with em. While I made croup tents with blankets and kettles of boilin water and rubbed their little chests with Vicks, Raymond prayed. He wasn't good at a whole lot of things, but he was awful good at prayin.

13

March 10, 1941 (Mon.) [Max 72°, Min 30°.]   Clear and sharply cool this morning, with the temperature down to 30° for the first light frost in 3 weeks, but another brilliantly clear, warm, glorious spring day. Yesterday's advanced summer-like heat has brought the first iris and other spring flowers into bloom and many fruit trees into blossom. Veda and I moved, with our family, into a nice new cabin on I Street today.

WARMER WEATHER CAME, and Raymond got promised several weeks of work helpin a farmer put in crops. I wanted our own place so bad I could taste it, and when Raymond told me there was some new cabins for rent over on I Street, I talked him into movin. He didn't want Laird to help us 'cause he didn't approve of his smokin and drinkin, but the folks he did approve of had helped us so many times I was embarrassed to ask em. Besides, I was tired of Raymond sayin, "I can't in good conscience," all the time. So I called Laird. He come with his car and hauled what we had from Mrs. Oliver's. Bea's husband brought over a davenport and a table and chairs they weren't usin, and after I put up curtains, the place looked real homey. But sometimes it seemed like the weather was against us. It had started out to be a nice warm spring, then it turned cold again and started rainin. The fields got muddy, and Raymond got laid off. Mrs. Oliver had already got somebody else to move into her place, so the only thing we could think to do was go back to Salem. Myrtle hadn't seen her grandbabies yet and I hoped she'd like havin em around.

We took Helena's room again, wedgin the kids' crib between the bed and the chest of drawers. Raymond got a job pickin beans with his dad and brothers, and my days were spent with Myrtle tellin me I didn't feed the kids right, I didn't dress em warm enough, and I was spoilin Rosalie. All the while she doted on Bubby, sayin how much he reminded her of Raymond.

In June we heard the strawberry farms was hirin pickers, so me and Raymond both signed up. I was nervous about leavin the kids with Myrtle all day, but we needed the money and I had to git away from her. It was hard work, squattin all day, duckwalkin up and down the rows, but it felt good to be outdoors. I picked twice as fast as Raymond did, so my pay was more, and at the end of the week we got two pay envelopes instead of one. I was almost sorry when it ended. I liked bein around the other pickers. Lots of em young like me, with husbands that didn't bring in enough to git by on.

I stayed on in Salem for the rest of the summer while Raymond followed crops. I got his letters regular as clockwork, each one sayin he was broke, the job he was on had ended, and he was movin on to some other place. And always, of course, the weather.

October 1, 1941 (Wed) [Max 64°, Min 43°.] Changeable and unsettled with light showers. I arrived at Troutdale today, found a room and then hunted up a job in the gladiola bulbs for a Mr. Burris. He has a house where I can live while working.

I tore Raymond's letter open and shook it. Nothin. I was really hopin for some money this time. His folks were feedin us, but the kids were growin like weeds and they needed shoes and clothes. Disappointed, I plopped down on a stump in the yard and started to read. He had been sick, he said, so he couldn't work. Said he used what money he had for stomach medicine and a place to sleep. Christ, what's goin to become of us? I kept readin, skippin over the weather report, lookin for some glimmer of hope. Then there it was. "...a new job in Troutdale ... keep me busy for several months ... a house as a part of my compensation." I read it again to make sure. He went on to say it was a nice area, beautiful country, on the Columbia River. I didn't care about none of that. What I cared about was the job. And the house!

"My boss will drive me to Salem and move our household goods for us. Have everything packed and be ready to leave on Sunday."

I grabbed Rosalie and whirled her round and round. She didn't know why her mama was happy, but she giggled and hugged me anyway. I started packin up right then and there. It didn't take me no time at all.

Raymond and his new boss pulled into the yard in a battered blue truck, and we were loaded up in minutes. Mr. Burris was a stocky older man. Real friendly with the kids. Teased Rosalie and put Bubby up next to him on the seat sayin he could help him drive. I could see right off he was a good man, willin to come all the way down to Salem, almost fifty miles, to git Raymond's family. And provide us a house, rent-free. I couldn't git over how lucky we were.

Mr. Burris talked while he drove, pointin out things, tellin us about his family and his business. After a time, he pulled the truck over to the side of the road and we got out. I'd brought sandwiches and a jar of milk for the kids. We had a little picnic and then we walked around to stretch our legs before goin on.

I was thrilled with the house, and Dorothy Burris turned out to be ever bit as nice as her husband. She come over with a big box of clothes and toys left from when her children were little. Said to let her know if there was anythin she could do to help me. Said she would be more than happy to drive me to town whenever I needed to go.

I wrote about it to Mama. How nice the Burrises were. How much I liked the house. My folks had sold the Cave Junction place and moved to Grants Pass. I missed them and wanted to see their new place, but for the first time since I got married it wasn't 'cause I didn't want to be where I was. We were better off than we'd ever been. Raymond had work. We had a house. I had my own kitchen. There was no Myrtle or Mrs. Oliver naggin at me, and I was really enjoyin my kids. They were beautiful, both of em. Smart and funny. Specially Rosalie. She made me laugh a dozen times a day.

Except for a few rides to town with Dorothy, I kept pretty much to myself, but it felt good knowin we had neighbors that would help out if we needed somethin. Mr. Burris, once in a while, would come by to ask how we was gittin on. He always stood awhile, visitin, bein friendly. One time Raymond seen me talkin to him and spent the whole night in a snit. Said I was flauntin myself. Said he seen me laugh and demanded to know what we were talkin about. I told him we was just visitin, that was all. I knew it upset him, but it wasn't like he thought. I told him Mr. Burris was a nice man and I wasn't goin to run and hide ever'time he come around, that as long as we was livin in his house and he was payin Raymond's wages, I was at least goin to be neighborly.

14

October 23, 1941 (Thurs.) [Max 57°, Min 40°.] Fair and cool all day with last evening's high cold wind from Mt. Hood's glacier continuing all day attaining an average velocity of from 25 to 35 miles per hour. A brand of weather to which I am unaccustomed, I worked in the bulbs in spite of the wind.

R AYMOND WASN'T HAPPY with what the job turned out to be. Mr. Burris expected him to work even when the wind blew, and if there was anythin Raymond hated, it was wind. But that wasn't what ended it.

Dorothy had give me a ride to town and seen how I was tryin to stretch the grocery money. She asked if her husband wasn't payin Raymond enough to feed his family. I told her that wasn't it. I said Mr. Burris was real generous, it was just that after Raymond paid our tithe to the church it left me short. I should of kept that to myself. She went right home and told her husband.

Mr. Burris jumped down from his truck, and started yellin at Raymond. "Jesus Christ, man, the reason I don't charge you rent on the god-damned house is so you'll have money to spend on your family. Buy groceries. Buy clothes for your kids. Get that pretty wife of yours a new dress. If you've got money to give away, I'll damn well start chargin you rent."

Well, Raymond wasn't goin to put up with nobody takin the Lord's name in vain like that, so he says, "I quit! I won't stick around and work for a man who uses that kind of language."

"Fine, quit if you want," Mr. Burris said, "but you ain't draggin Veda and them babies along while you look for a new job. You leave them here until you find work and a decent place to live."

Raymond didn't argue, he just turned around and went in the house. I stood there and watched my world fall down around me. This was the first good job Raymond'd had and I was so happy when he got it. Now he'd gone and quit without givin me and the kids a thought. Tears stung my eyes. Raymond already had it in his head there was somethin between Mr. Burris and me, and I knew I should refuse Mr. Burris's offer to stay, but I had the kids to think about. It was clear that Mr. Burris, who barely knew me, cared more about us than my husband did. Raymond left the next mornin, vowin to send for us as soon as he found work. Swore he wasn't goin to leave us with a "blasphemer" any longer'n he had to.

October 30, 1941 (Thurs.) [Max 60°, Min 38°.] Mostly clear all this a.m. following the coolest morning we have had this fall, becoming hazy and cloudy this p.m. but remaining quite cool until late. I left the Burris place this a.m. and I have found a job picking up potatoes. I will be getting 40 cents an hour instead of the 30 cents I was getting from Mr.

Burris. I expect to start tomorrow.

Landin a job that paid better was sort of like thumbin his nose at Mr. Burris, but I wasn't dumb enough to think the ten-cent difference made up for losin the house. Then after crowin about the better wages, Raymond wrote to tell me the weather was bad and he wasn't gittin much work after all.

The dollars dribbled in from Raymond a few at a time, always with a letter sayin he was barely makin enough to keep himself fed and he couldn't see his way clear to find us a place to live. I knew how lucky I was we had a roof over our heads, but I needed money to buy groceries. I decided to ask Dorothy Burris if she had some work I could do.

When I seen the little bit of ironin, I knew she was just bein charitable when she said she couldn't keep up. Raymond could say what he wanted about the Burrises, but I thought they were the most Christian people I ever come across. Instead of thinkin themselves better than other people the way Raymond did, they helped folks out. Like givin Raymond the job in the first place. Givin us a place to live. Carin about us. I thought a lot about that, and about what bein a Christian meant. Was Raymond bein a good Christian by turnin down work in order to keep the Sabbath? By despisin folks that used tobacco and alcohol? By quittin a perfectly good job 'cause his boss blasphemed? Wasn't providin for his children somethin a Christian ought to do?

Me and the kids started spendin a couple mornins a week in Dorothy Burris's kitchen where I felt safe and welcome. While she made bread or pies, I ironed. I sprinkled the pieces with water from a Coke bottle and rolled em up. Then, pullin one piece at a time from the basket, I'd run the iron over it till I had it all perfect. I liked the hiss of the hot iron and the sweet, hot smell of steam. The radio would be playin and I'd lose myself in the back and forth rhythm. Smoothin, foldin, pressin, and foldin again. Rosalie got up on a stool beside Dorothy to help roll pie dough, and Bubby played on the floor with lids. Ever since Mr. Burris held him behind the steerin wheel of his truck, Bubby's favorite game was pretendin to drive.

"Mithter Burrith is a blathphemer," Rosalie blurted out one mornin. I stopped halfway up the side of a pillowcase, my face on fire, and tried to think of somethin to say. I couldn't git after her, she was just repeatin what she heard.

"I'm so sorry," I said to Mrs. Burris. "She's just… Raymond didn't… I mean… What he meant was…"

Dorothy wiped her hands on her apron and set down. She looked at Rosalie for a long time. Then she started laughin. She laughed and laughed till there was tears rollin down her cheeks.

15

December 7, 1941 (Sun.) [Max 48°, Min 37°.] Clear, fair and cool all day with chilly east-to-northeast wind, Clear and colder at night and still, wind has moved into the north so we will probably have a hard freeze before morning, Japanese bombed Pearl Harbor, Hawaii, this morning.

IT WAS IN DOROTHY'S KITCHEN that I heard the news about Pearl Harbor. Me and her set at the table, leanin close to the radio, listnin to Edward R. Murrow and Gabriel Heatter, the hiss and crackle makin it seem like the war was right there in the kitchen with us. I kept thinkin how my troubles were nothin compared to all them women that lost their husbands and would have to raise their children alone. Or the ones plannin to be married that wouldn't git the chance. I couldn't git over how awful it was.

Raymond come back to the house a couple days before Christmas, out of work and with just enough money in his pocket for a few groceries. Mr. Burris must of knew he was there, but he didn't come over. Dorothy did, though, and if it wasn't for the presents she brought for the kids, they wouldn't of had none. Raymond told me to send em back. Said he didn't want his children gittin gifts bought with a blasphemer's money. I asked him what he thought we were livin on all this time. "It's Christmas," I said, "and the kids are keepin these presents. If you take that little bit of pleasure away from em, I'll never speak to you again."

January 12, 1942 (Mon.) [Max 31°, Min 19°.] Severely cold again today, also rather cloudy and overcast, with wind, which makes this the bitterest cold spell I have ever experienced and it finds us without fuel, groceries or lights, even without water until 3 days ago.

The new year started off with a blizzard. Electric lines were down and the pipes froze. We were out of wood and the house was so cold I was havin to wrap the kids up in blankets. I begged Raymond to go up to Burris's and borrow some wood so I could cook, but he paced, slappin his arms, and blowin on his hands, and wouldn't budge. I was disgusted. He'd been gone for almost two months while we lived hand to mouth, and now he was back actin like a spoiled baby.

"Why in God's name can't you at least go and ask?" I yelled at him.

"I won't deal with a blasphemer," he said.

I was shakin, I was so mad. His children were cold and hungry and all he cared about was his principles.

"Don't you care about anybody but yourself?" I screamed steppin toward him. He raised his arm to keep me back, and his hand hit my nose. It started to bleed.

"If you won't go, I will." I grabbed his work coat and gloves off the hook and pushed the door against the wind. The Burris's house was about two hundred yards from our place and the snow was blowin so hard I could barely see. I tried to walk, but I kept fallin. Finally I stayed down and crawled.

"What the hell happened," Mr. Burris asked when he opened the door, "did you fall?"

"I need to borrow some wood."

"You're bleeding," he said. "He didn't hit you, did he? Did that little weasel hit you?"

"I'm all right," I said. "He's just upset. It's my fault, I was yellin at him."

"Like hell it is!" he shouted. "I'll show that sonofabitch a thing or two."

"No, please don't," I said. "He didn't do it on purpose."

Mr. Burris wasn't listenin. He threw a bunch of wood on a sled and told me to git on. Then he pulled me back up to the house. Raymond was on his knees prayin, and when he saw who was with me, he started scootin backwards. That's when Mr. Burris grabbed him by the collar, held him up, and punched him. Raymond fell backwards and Mr. Burris turned to me.

"Are you going to be all right?"

I nodded. He turned again to Raymond. "If you touch her again, I'll see you locked up."

I built a fire and fixed the kids some supper while Raymond sat, crumpled up like a wad of paper. His lip started to swell, but I was too angry to care. I knew he hadn't meant to hit me, but he could of said he was sorry. Not just for bloodyin my nose, but for bein such a pitiful excuse for a father.

The storm went on for more than a week, and all the while Raymond paced like a caged animal. When it finally let up, he hitched a ride into town with a delivery truck driver. "I'll let you know when I find a job," he said. "And I fully intend to report Mr. Burris's assault to the police."

April 12, 1942 (Sun.) [Max 71°, Min 25°.] Clear and warm, a perfect day, the third fine, warm Sunday in succession. This has certainly been a beautiful April so far. I have a new job in Canby, so I have located an apartment and paid a week's rent on it.

Raymond wrote to say he had a job and had rented a furnished apartment, so Mr. Burris drove me and the kids to Canby. I didn't like the looks of the town. Canneries, packin plants and railroad tracks. The apartment was in a rundown two-story clapboard with a cattywampus front porch. Rickety stairs leaned against one side of the house, and thick green moss covered the roof like a blanket. Mr. Burris stayed in the truck with the kids while I went to the door.

"You Mrs. Ames?" The man who answered my knock asked. When I nodded, he pointed at the stairs. "It's up there. Your husband said to let you in."

I followed him, holdin on to the handrail. He pushed the door open and the smell of urine and mildew almost knocked me over. There was one big room with cracked linoleum, water stains on the ceilin and walls, and two filthy windows. An iron cookstove and a washbasin stood in one corner. I wondered if Raymond had even looked at it.

"That there's the kitchen," he said, "and that bucket's for fetchin water." He turned to leave. "Them your younguns in the truck? I hope they's quiet."

I went down the stairs and got the kids, and Mr. Burris started bringin up my things. "Veda," he said, lookin around, "you know you don't have to do this. You can stay with us as long as you need to."

I felt like cryin. I wanted nothin more than to git back in the truck and return to where we had a decent house and good people to look out for us. But I couldn't. Raymond was my husband and he'd got us this place to live. I knew I had to stay.

It was supposed to be furnished, but there was only a metal bedstead with a dirty mattress, a table with two chairs, and a freestandin cupboard. For a closet there was just some brackets nailed to the wall with two shelf boards and a broomstick between em. I looked around for a place to put Bubby down. I didn't want him on that filthy floor and I knew it would take Raymond the better part of a day to set up the crib. I spread my coat on the linoleum, put Bubby on it, and told Rosalie to make sure he stayed there.

"Good," Raymond said when he showed up and saw us. "I brought some groceries." He set the sack down and kissed the kids.

I'd seen a woodpile by the stairs when I come up, so I sent Raymond back outside to git some, then I built a fire in the stove and sent him to fetch water. When the water was hot, I started to clean and Raymond went to work settin up the crib. The room got warm and the smell of Purex covered up the other odors. Bubby fell asleep and Rosalie started to sing, "Wock a bye baby, in the twee top" to her doll.

I found a roll of shelf paper in one of the boxes I'd brung with me, white with tiny blue and pink flowers, so I got my scissors and started linin shelves. I finished one and bent down to pick up another sheet of paper, and when I stood up, I hit my head on the cupboard door.

"Goddammit!" The words hung in the air like smoke.

"Oh, no, no, Veda," Raymond said, comin to stand over me. "You mustn't take the Lord's name in vain."

"I'm sorry," I said.

"You need to pray, Veda. Say, 'Get thee behind me Satan.'"

"Git thee behind me Satan," I mumbled.

"Say it again."

"Git thee behind me Satan."

I was mad enough to spit nails and I knew Raymond knew it. When I bumped my head a second time and "Goddammit" slipped out of my mouth again, he give me that sad, "my wife is goin to hell" look, but he didn't say a word to me about prayin.

I despised that apartment. A dozen times a day I had to take the stairs to "fetch" water or bring up wood. Bubby was always gittin over close to the stove and there was only Rosalie to watch him. I was scared to death he'd git burnt.

We were only there a couple weeks before Raymond lost his job. I was furious. I knew he couldn't help bein laid off, but if he hadn't been in such a damn hurry to git us away from Mr. Burris, he could of made sure the job was goin to last.

Raymond left us there and went back to trampin from place to place, pickin up whatever odd job he could git. He'd be gone for five or ten days, then turn up out of the blue. Rosalie always warmed up to him right away, but poor little Bubby didn't. He'd bury his head in my shoulder or hide behind my skirt, and it took longer ever'time for him to git used to his daddy.

Raymond couldn't seem to keep any job. Sometimes

it was 'cause he wouldn't work on the Sabbath, and other times it was 'cause the job shut down. I managed to pay rent and buy some groceries with the little money he sent but, like ever one else, I had to use ration stamps. I didn't mind doin my part for the war effort, but the stamps confused me. I had a awful time keepin track of how many points it took to buy a can of peas or a sack of flour, or how much sugar you was allowed. Me and the kids lived on Carnation milk, Cream of Wheat, and canned peaches, and I tried to keep enough food in the house so when Raymond showed up there would be somethin for him to eat.

Those ration stamps were about the only connection I had to the war. Raymond wasn't in it, and since I didn't have a radio, I didn't know what was goin on. Mama wrote me about President Roosevelt's fireside talks, but I never heard em. When I went to the store, I sometimes seen the newspaper headlines. Always spellin out JAPS in big ugly black letters. None of it seemed real to me. Once I bought a newspaper and read about the Japanese Americans bein put in camps. I thought it was awful, but the whole country was scared I guess.

Bea wrote that Rheba and Flossie had got married to the Loemen brothers, Howard and Ira, in a quick ceremony at the courthouse. Two weddins at once. The brothers had both joined the army and were bein sent overseas.

Livin in Canby would of been unbearable without my kids. Bubby with his husky laugh and Rosalie sayin all her cute and funny words. She liked to sing and I taught her ever song I could think of. "Down in the Meadee in a Iddy Biddy Poo," "Itsy Bitsy Spider," "I

Love You a Bushel and a Peck." We sang "Ring around the Rosie, pocket full a posies, ashes, ashes, all fall down," and collapsed on the floor in giggles. And ever'time we made any kind of noise, that old devil downstairs pounded on the ceilin with what I imagined to be the handle of his pitchfork.

Sometimes the things Rosalie said left me not knowin whether to laugh or cry. Once when I went for water and come flyin back up the stairs, she was on her knees in front of her brother. She had her head bowed and her eyes closed.

"Git ahind me Satan, dammit," she said, "git ahind me Satan, dammit."

I had to go back out the door so she wouldn't see me laugh. It got my attention, though, seein her repeat what she heard like that. I had this bad habit of mumblin to myself about Raymond, how he ought to be workin instead a prayin, how he wasn't never around when I needed him. But seein what a copycat Rosalie was turnin into, I started tryin real hard to keep my thoughts to myself. I knew I'd be in big trouble if she repeated any of what I said in front of her daddy.

Our place didn't have a yard and there wasn't a park or nothin close by, so the only time we got out was when we went to the store. If it was rainin, I bundled Bubby into the buggy and dressed Rosalie in her coat and rubber boots. I loved watchin her run and jump and dance through the mud puddles. But at night I was scared. We were only a block from the railroad tracks, and I could see hobo camps in the bushes from my window. It give me the creeps, them bein so close and me and the kids alone most of the time. And I hated the trains. I felt like they was runnin my life. The 7:00 a.m. was my alarm clock, I put the kids down for naps after the 2:15, and the one that come screamin through at 3:00 in the mornin gave me nightmares.

16

August 17, 1942 (Mon.) [Max. 87°, Min. 50°.] Continued clear and hot, but more breezy and tolerable. We picked hops again today. Our little boy's 2nd birthday. I bought him some cake and ice cream this evening. His poor little face is badly sunburned from the hot sun in the hop yards.

HOP VINES HUNG LIKE rugs on a clothesline. I hadn't wanted to bring the kids along, but there wasn't anybody to watch em. I put Bubby on a blanket in the only shade I could find and told Rosalie she had to keep an eye on him. Then I went and got a basket and started to pick, lookin back over my shoulder ever few minutes.

They're funny little things, hops. The size of a man's thumb and sticky. The best way to pick em is to grab ahold of the vine and pull down real fast so a bunch of em come off at a time. By noon my back ached and I had big white blisters on my hands. I looked over at the kids. They weren't in the shade any more. Bubby's hat was off and his little face was red as a beet. I turned around. Raymond was a couple rows behind me, pickin the hops off one at a time, singin, "Jesus loves me" (plop) "this I know" (plop), like a kid on a Sabbath School picnic. I finished fillin the basket I had and went to check on the kids. I'd already turned in four baskets and Raymond hadn't even filled two. At this rate, we'd be lucky to make six dollars between us.

When we got home I was so pooped I could barely move, but I managed to fix supper. Poor little Bubby was so tired and sunburnt, he fell asleep eatin his birthday cake. I hated the thought of takin the kids back to that field again, but we signed on to pick, so we didn't have a choice.

When the landlord upped the rent to thirty dollars, Raymond told him we wouldn't be stayin. Said he had a hunch he could get work shakin prunes in Roseburg. I should git the kids ready and we'd go down on the Greyhound Bus.

I was so sick of livin in that apartment I was willin to go just about anyplace, and besides, Roseburg was closer to my folks. Raymond wanted to ask his brother Norman to drive up and git our things, but I didn't want Norman usin his gas rations to do us a favor. Nothin we had was worth it. We put as much as we could in the baby buggy, filled the suitcases, and left the rest.

I had on my one good dress, Raymond was wearin his Sabbath suit, and the kids were clean and combed and pretty, and when I seen our reflection in a store window, it stopped me in my tracks. I'd forgot what a handsome family we were. I threw my shoulders back and felt good clear up to the minute I stepped off the bus in Roseburg and got hit in the face with the smell.

"What's that stink?" I asked Raymond.

He said it was comin from the mill and I'd git used to it. I put my hand over my nose and looked around. Wigwam burners spewed smoke, and logs rotted in float ponds. I wondered if this was such a good idea after all.

We walked for a long ways before Raymond stopped in front of a old brick buildin with a sign that said GRAND HOTEL and put the suitcases down. There was a heavy door and two big windows that looked like they hadn't been washed in years.

"Is this where we're stayin?" I asked. "They've a lot a nerve callin it grand."

"It'll only be a few days."

The place gave me the creeps, and so did the old man that hobbled over to take our bags. He bent down and grabbed our suitcases, and we followed him up a staircase that smelled like the town, only worse.

In the mornin Raymond got a newspaper and went to look for a place to rent. He come back all excited, sayin he found a nice apartment. "Only sixteen dollars, and the lady said we can have it for twelve if I split wood and keep the furnace stoked."

I couldn't believe it. Twelve dollars was what the dump in Grants Pass had cost. This place was clean and modern. Even had carpet. It was ever bit as nice as what Bea and them had, and I wished Mama could see it. For days, I walked around touchin the nubby, dark pink davenport, the polished wood tables, the drapes, almost afraid to breathe. I kept expectin the lady to see her mistake and tell us to leave.

And Raymond was right about Roseburg. I got used to the smoke and the smell, and he found work in the prune harvest. His new boss was Adventist, too, so he didn't have to work on the Sabbath. I wrote to Mama and Bea tellin em about our place and about Raymond's new job. It lasted for almost two whole months, until the telegram came sayin Raymond's dad had suffered a stroke, so Raymond drew his pay and we headed back to Salem.

It was a sad time after Nathaniel died. Even with the others there to help out, Myrtle clung to Raymond. I felt bad for her, but I wanted us to git back to our own life. The lady in Roseburg said she'd hold the apartment for us, but she didn't say for how long.

When we got back the prune harvest was over, so even though the apartment was waitin for us, the job wasn't. I was tired of bein parked in one town while Raymond worked in another one. Besides, I was pregnant again and in no shape to be choppin wood and stokin furnaces. So Raymond sent us back to live with Mama in Grants Pass and he went off to Canyonville, where he heard there was work prunin trees. That didn't last either. He showed up broke three weeks later and moved in with me at Mama's.

Papa was fed up. "That boy's just plain pitiful," he said. "He's got two kids and a third on the way, and it don't look like he's ever gonna show any gumption."

With Papa's proddin, Raymond went to the railroad office and got hired as a section hand. I didn't know what a section hand was, but I didn't care. It was a real job and it paid sixty-five cents an hour. I was thrilled. He would go off in the mornin like my sisters' husbands, and come back at night. He'd have a regular paycheck, and we'd be able to stay in Grants Pass.

We got us a house. A big, drafty place that some folks from the church let us have cheap. It wasn't as nice as the Roseburg place, but it was close to my folks on a good-size piece of land. It had a big yard for the kids to play in, and there was even a pear orchard that hadn't been took care of for years. Raymond was excited about the trees. He knew all about prunin. Said we'd have us a good crop by summer.

17

March 21, 1943 (Sun.) [Max 64°, Min 37°.] Cloudy all day but mild and balmy with a southerly breeze. A beautiful spring day, with green grass, yellow daffodils, swelling green buds and pink blossoms on the Japanese flowering cherry trees. Our baby daughter, weighing 7½ lbs., was born at the Josephine County Hospital this morning.

RUTH ANN ARRIVED ON the first day of spring. A healthy baby with a full head of dark hair. Like Rosalie, she was bright and alert, not colicky, and except for all the extra laundry, no trouble at all. When I was feelin good enough, I started takin the kids outside to git fresh air and sunshine. I put Ruthie in the buggy and let the other two play in the yard while I hung laundry on the clothesline. The hills around us were green, the trees in our little orchard were blossomed out, and the air smelled wonderful. I loved spring.

We settled into a routine. Raymond went to work early and came home while it was still light. He took Rosalie and Bubby on walks and told em the names of plants and flowers. Took em out to the orchard to visit the trees. Bubby loved to follow his daddy around, wearin his hat and carryin his lunch bucket. It made me happy seein Raymond with the kids that way. Made me think ever'thin was goin to be all right.

I was glad to be close to my folks and my sisters. And, since I didn't have a washin machine of my own, I was specially glad to be close enough to use Mama's Maytag. Wash day was my favorite time of the whole week. I packed kids and dirty clothes in the baby buggy and went down the hill to Mama's. I liked bein there in her kitchen with the steamy smell of Fels Naptha soap and the sleepy chuga-chuga of the washin machine. Rosalie would be on the floor with her color book, her soft curls fallin across her face. Bubby usually found some lids to play with, and baby Ruthie'd be asleep in the buggy. I'd turn the radio on and sing along to "Boogie Woogie Bugle Boy" or "Is You Is Or Is You Ain't My Baby." I knew the words to all the songs, but I couldn't sing em at home 'cause it was "worldly" and Raymond didn't approve.

Then the news would come on and I'd feel awful. Hearin about all those soldiers gittin killed. Boys eighteen, nineteen years old. Married men. Daddies that wouldn't ever git to see their children. Made me feel guilty for havin a husband safe at home while all those others—Rheba's and Flossie's husbands, and most of the young men from our church—were overseas fightin the war. And the other thing I felt guilty about was wishin, sometimes, that Raymond would git drafted.

He had a job. I couldn't complain about that. And we had a decent place to live now. But he never lifted a finger to help me. On Sabbath I'd git so mad at him I wanted to scream. He'd git himself ready for church. Put on the clothes I laid out for him, the shoes I polished. He'd shave, oil his hair, then set by the door with his Bible and his hat, tappin his foot and tellin me to hurry while I cooked his breakfast, nursed the baby, got Rosalie and Bubby dressed and fed, fixed Rosalie's hair, and tried to make myself presentable. Then there was the long walk, him struttin on ahead with Rosalie while I struggled with the two babies in a wobbly-wheeled buggy. Once in a while someone would take pity on us and give us a ride, and grateful as I was to not have to walk, that made me mad too. I hated to be beholden.

18

MY PAPA DIED THE SPRING after Ruthie was born. It was a real blow to all of us. He'd been ornery, but he wasn't sick. Then all of a sudden he took to his bed with a cough that kept gittin worse. The doctor come to the house and give Mama all sorts of potions and whatnot, but it was like Papa just give up. Wasn't but a few days and he was gone. Mama took it awful hard. They been together forty-five years.

I was the youngest and, I think, Papa's favorite. When I was little, he took me with him to do chores and check on the sheep. He taught me to ride horses and spit, and I learned my first cuss words from him. Got my mouth washed out with soap more'n once for it. Mama took over once I started school, makin sure I learned manners, but I never forgot how it was with Papa and me when I was little. I missed him somethin terrible.

I thought about the stories Papa used to tell. And how he could always make me laugh. He told me how things were way back before he had a family. About his cowboy days when he was herdin sheep across

Montana and Wyomin, only gittin off his horse at night, sleepin on the ground, and eatin nothin but canned beans and hardtack. I liked to imagine him that way. Young and handsome, not all crippled up.

He told me stories about my brothers when they was younger. About George gittin trampled by his horse, and Wilbert bein throwed by a bull. I loved the way he told the stories, usin his whole body, actin ever'thin out. One minute he'd be buckin like the bull and the next pretendin to be Wil hangin on for dear-life. He told stories about my sisters too. One about Bea hidin the dirty dishes in the oven 'cause her fella showed up before she got em washed, and them burnin up when Mama lit the stove. Papa told that one so many times I thought I remembered it myself.

I specially loved it when he talked about the old Indian woman he called Leet-ivy. He'd always chuckle a bit, then lean way back in his chair. "She was a funny old thing," he'd say. "Bout a hundred years old. Didn't have a tooth in her head. The only white people words she knew was cuss words and my name.

"That old woman. Git right up in my face and go to spoutin gibberish I couldn't no more figure out than nothin. Like her name, we never knew for sure. Said it over and over. Somethin that sounded like 'Leet-ivy, Leet-ivy,' so that's what we called her. Couldn't tell what it was she wanted neither. She'd jabber somethin and then holler, 'Goddamn ya, Miles,' and jabber some more. I'd smile and wait for her to wear herself out."

Mama got after Papa, sayin it was mean to make fun of the poor old thing that way, but I loved the stories and I begged Papa to keep goin.

"She was always wrapped up in one a them Injun blankets. Had so many bones and teeth rattlin round her neck we could hear her comin a mile off. Wore a dirty ole pair a moccasins with rags hangin out the back. Brung us things, dead rabbits, squirrels. Your ma, she give Leet-ivy coins, pretty rocks, old pieces a cloth. Then after she rode off, we buried the varmints. Sure as hell wasn't goin to cook em. One time me and the boys was in the barn when she come in and started carryin on. I was shoein a horse and I just kept poundin, tryin to drown her out. Wilbert and George snuck up behind her and drove nails into them shoe-rags of hers. I could see what they was up to, but with all the hammerin, Leet-ivy didn't notice. When she tries to leave and sees she's nailed down, she goes to cussin a blue streak. The boys near-bout bust a gut laughin.

"She was skinny as a starved jackrabbit," Papa said. "Couldn't eat, I 'magine, havin no teeth an all. One day she shows up and gives me this big ol' smile. I can see her gums is all red and swoll up and she's got her jaws clamped down on a set of the awfullest lookin choppers you ever seen. Holy Christ, I says to myself, she's gone and stuck a bear's teeth up in her gums. I knew she'd die of blood poisonin if I didn't get em out a her mouth, so I put her up on old Blacky, the meanest sonofabitch horse I had. He went crazy, buckin and rearin, and ever'time old Leet-ivy opened her mouth to holler, 'Goddamn ya, Miles,' some a them teeth fell out."

19

February 23, 1945 (Fri.) [Max 52°, Min 35°.] Chilly, unsettled and changeable here in Portland, with raw wind and light showers intermingled with sunshine. I had my pre-induction physical examination this morning which resulted in my rejection from military service at this time.

RAYMOND GOT A LETTER from the draft board sayin he had to go to Portland for a physical examination. I held my breath. He wasn't the soldierin type. He hated guns and war, of course, but he also hated the idea of bein around men that didn't live the kind of clean and godly life he lived. For him it would of been worse than the WPA. That letter scared him, and before he left for Portland, he took us to have a family picture made. "If I have to go to war," he said, "I want there to be a photograph of me and my family."

So we got this picture. There's Raymond in his dark Sabbath suit and me in a nice dress somebody give me. It's dark blue and has a pretty lace collar. Rosalie's wearin a flowered pinafore, her hair in ringlets, Bubby looks like a serious little man with his striped shirt and suspenders, and Ruthie's a little china doll propped up in front of me. My pregnancy doesn't show.

Raymond didn't git drafted after all. They told him he had ulcers. He'd always had stomach trouble but didn't know what caused it. Now that he knew what it was, he complained even more. He started missin work, comin home midday all doubled over. His paychecks got smaller and smaller. I felt bad for him, but I wasn't well either. I was six months pregnant, my feet were swole up, and my back hurt. Besides that, the doctor said I had iron poor blood. Told me to eat liver to build myself up. He knew I was a vegetarian, but said I couldn't afford to take chances with my health and the baby's.

That didn't set well with Raymond. My eatin liver was somethin he wouldn't stand for. To him, it was a matter of conscience. When I said that to Mama, she hit the ceilin.

"Raymond can do what he wants with his conscience," she said. "But this is about you and that baby." She started buyin liver and cookin it for me whenever I come to her house. It tasted nasty and had a awful smell, but I gagged it down. When I told her Raymond was goin to be mad, she said, "Raymond doesn't need to know."

April 13, 1945 (Fri.) [Max. 52°, Min. 28°.] A record cold morning for Mid-April with a persistent, biting wind. I left work at mid-morning due to my stomach trouble. Veda met with an accident which may necessitate an operation. She was removed to the hospital and I am very much concerned. I shall hope and pray that an operation may not be necessary to save her and the baby.

The wind blew all night and was still whistlin in the mornin when I went out to sweep the leaves and branches off the porch. It was cold. I pulled my sweater tight around me and held it with my forearms while I worked the broom. My feet were swole up like balloons, so I had on a old pair of Raymond's shoes. A pile of leaves blew up into my face, and when I stopped to rub my eyes I seen Raymond comin up the hill all hunched over. I knew how much he hated workin out in the wind, but the month wasn't even half over and he'd missed four days already. I could feel the bile raisin up in my throat.

"What happened?" I asked when he reached the porch.

"It's too cold," he said. "I can't work in this."

"You can't NOT work! We won't be able to pay the rent. We can't afford for you to take time off."

"Leave me alone," he said. "My ulcer is acting up. I'm in no condition to work."

"No condition!" I yelled. "NO CONDITION! What kind of condition do you think I'm in?"

He started to go in the house, and I grabbed at his coat.

"Leave me alone," he said, givin me a shove.

I felt myself fallin, grabbin at the air. I landed on my stomach at the bottom of the steps and couldn't git my breath. I tasted copper.

Raymond was beside me then, sayin, "I'm sorry, I'm so sorry. I didn't mean to..." He carried me in the house and started dabbin at my legs with a washrag. I felt a rush of somethin wet. I sent Rosalie for a towel and shoved it between my legs. It turned red with blood. "Call the doctor!" I screamed. "Call the goddamned doctor!"

I was in the hospital for a week and was told that I had to stay off my feet or I could lose the baby. I couldn't go home because there was no one there to help me, so I went to stay with Mama. We were there for the next six weeks. Mama took care of my kids.

I prayed a lot through that whole time, askin God to tell me what to do. I knew Raymond didn't mean to hurt me. Like that time at Burris's place when he hit me and bloodied my nose. I was yellin at him and all he wanted was to be left alone. I never did think he was mean. I just thought he was weak. And I didn't know how we were ever goin to survive with him bein that way.

20

June 3, 1945 (Sun.) [Max. 75°, Min. 42°.] Quite cool in morning; partly cloudy today, but pleasantly warm, A nice sunny day. Our fourth child, a son, was born at the hospital at 3:30 p.m. today, weighing 8 lbs. 2oz.

RAYMOND BARELY CAME to see me while I was laid up at Mama's, but he showed up at the hospital after the baby was born. He acted peevish and didn't have any suggestions about a name. Said he'd leave it up to me. I thought about the ordeal this baby had went through and decided he needed a strong name. Like Samson in the Bible. Samson, I liked that. I'd call him Sam.

I was the opposite of strong. I had lost a lot of blood and was too weak to do much of anythin, let alone take care of four kids without help. So Mama said I should come back to her house and she would watch the kids. Raymond come by the first couple of Sabbaths and took Rosalie and Bubby to church. But after that he stopped comin around.

It was a month before I felt strong enough to go

home, and by then I'd got myself all balled up inside tryin to decide if I wanted to. I couldn't stop thinkin about how spineless Raymond was. About all his excuses, the things he wouldn't do 'cause of his conscience, the way we lived, and the way we would keep on livin.

And it really bothered me that he called what happened an accident. He didn't mean to push me, but at least he could own up to doin it, not go around sayin, "Veda had an accident." What if somethin like that happened again? What if I got hurt even worse? My kids needed me. And they needed food and clothes and a decent place to live. Needed that ever bit as much as they needed Raymond's Christlike example.

When we got married, he promised to take care of me, but it seemed like the only one he was takin care of was himself. And he wasn't even doin a decent job of that. If he wasn't willin to take responsibility for me and for his children, I would have to. It was a hard decision. One minute I was thinkin of him as a self-servin sonofabitch, and the next I was tellin myself it wasn't fair to deprive the kids of their father. I was scared to death. But in the long run, stayin with him seemed riskier than leavin.

I might of lost my nerve if Raymond hadn't helped me make up my mind. It was a Sunday night and I had the kids bedded down on Mama's davenport. I was readin em a story and nursin Sam, when Raymond showed up.

"Where've you been?" I asked. "Were you workin overtime?"

"They gave me a week's vacation."

"Oh?"

He lowered his head and reached for Rosalie.

"So why didn't you come down and see the kids?"

"I went to see Mother."

"Is she sick?"

"No, I just—"

"And you didn't tell me you were goin?"

"No, I—"

"How long did you stay?"

He said he spent a couple of days in Salem and then his brother Norman drove em over to the coast for the rest of the week.

"Over to the coast? You stayed over at the coast? What did that cost?"

He studied his shoes.

"We're here livin off Mama, and you spend money on a vacation at the beach. What on earth were you thinkin?" I could hear my voice gittin that high screechy sound, and I knew I better stop or I'd grab him by the throat. "I've got a headache," I said. "You better leave."

21

July 24, 1945 (Tue.) [Max. 92°, Min. 51°.] Clear and much cooler this morning, remaining clear and becoming sweltering hot for the beginning of another scorching midsummer heat wave. Second crop of clover hay is now being harvested. Veda has sued me for divorce.

I JUST CAN'T CONDONE IT." Mama said. Raymond's uselessness was as big a thorn in her side as it was in mine, but she was dead set against divorce. "You made a promise to God, Veda, for richer or poorer, for better or worse."

"I know Mama, but how much worse? We're livin here under your roof and Raymond's never give us a dime. He doesn't even come to see the kids. I've made up my mind. I'm not goin back."

Raymond didn't even try to talk me out of it. He quit his good job with the railroad job and went cryin to his mother. Told her he had worked so hard to provide for his dear little family. Prayed not to be drafted for their sake. Sacrificed so much, only to have his wife commit adultery and sue him for a divorce.

I was furious. When in hell would I have committed adultery? When I was takin care of his kids? Cookin his meals? Doin his laundry? Or when I was in the hospital after he pushed me down the stairs?

Of course his mother believed ever word and got him a lawyer, a man from her church in Salem who probably didn't charge her.

They took me to court and Raymond's mother did most of the talkin. Some ladies from our church's Dorcas Society came to speak up for him too. Tried their damnedest, all of em, to git my kids away from me. They said I was a bad mother. Said I hadn't been in church in months. Even though they knew about the accident, knew I was laid up all that time. They said Raymond was the one who was fit to raise the children. Said how clean and well-mannered the children were when he brought em to church. Who did they think was takin care of em? One woman had the gall to say she seen me take milk from my babies and drink it myself.

It turned into a kind of Adventist circus, with me in front of the judge shakin so bad I almost couldn't answer his questions. When I was asked about the adultery charge, I started to cry. I told him it wasn't true. That I couldn't have … that I was sick and stayin at my mother's house, and that Raymond hadn't been to see me or the children durin the whole time. That he hadn't give me any support at all.

The judge looked disgusted. He give me custody of the kids and ordered Raymond to pay a hundred dollars a month for child support. Raymond said it wasn't fair. Said Oregon law was biased toward mothers, even undeservin ones like me.

I don't think Raymond wanted custody anyhow.

He couldn't support em when he had me to take care of ever'thin, so how could he do it alone. They would of ended up stayin with his mother. And the idea of her raisin my kids was downright scary.

August 28, 1945 (Tue.) [Max. 96°, Min. 54°.] Scorching hot and dry as we reach the peak of another brief late summer heat wave. Second sweltering Tuesday in succession and I really suffered with the heat both days at my job. Veda's divorce has gone through.

I got a lot of letters from Raymond but, most of the time, instead of sendin money, he sent excuses. Work was hard to find, he said, and most places wouldn't hire him unless he joined a union which his conscience wouldn't let him do. Loyalty to anythin other than God was against his religious principles. Every month it was the same thing. No child support. He begged me not to turn him in. I wouldn't have anyway. I just didn't have the heart.

The things that were said about me spread through the church like a house afire. I'd walk in on Sabbath mornin with the kids all scrubbed and smilin, and them Dorcas Society ladies would purse their lips and tighten their butt cheeks and whisper loud enough so I couldn't help but hear.

"Tramp ... robbin that fine Christian man of his sweet children ... last baby is probably not even his..."

But while the women were stickin up their noses, their husbands were sniffin around me like hogs at a slop bucket. Could they help me with anythin? Drive me someplace? Do anythin for me at all? I stopped goin. Mama kept after me, sayin they were havin a field day. Said ever'time I didn't show up it give em even more to talk about.

"They can all go to hell," I said. "They'll say them things anyhow and I'm not goin to go to church and be treated that way." And I didn't go back either, not for a long time.

With so little money comin from Raymond, I had to rely on Mama and the little bit I made doin ironin and sellin donuts three or four dozen at a time. I got up early to make the donuts and then my brother Laird delivered em to this little breakfast place downtown. It was a lot of work, and after buyin flour and sugar and Crisco, I wasn't comin out much ahead. I knew I needed a real job, but I didn't know where to look. Then I found out the box factory was hirin girls so I went to see if I could git on. They wanted to know if I could stand on my feet all day and lift forty pounds. I told em it couldn't be any harder than packin babies around. The job was six days a week so I'd have to work Saturdays. I didn't think God would mind.

The first day was real bad. The boss lady took me through the plant and showed me what I was supposed to do. There was this thing called a conveyor belt. It carried cardboard that was cut and folded flat, and I was to take em from where they got dumped in a chute and stack em on a pallet behind me. It sounded easier than it was. They come down that belt lickety-split and I couldn't git em out fast enough. Git jammed up and boxes'd go ever whichaway.

There was this big fat girl at the next machine, and ever'time she seen me gittin behind, she come over. Never said a blessed word to me, just jerked things out of my hands and shoved me out of the way. Then once she got me caught up, she'd go back to her own side. I would of thanked her for helpin if she'd been nice about it.

When the dinner bell rang they shut the conveyor down, and the whole bunch of women went over to where some tables was pushed up together. They was all talkin amongst themselves, ignorin me, so I went to a empty table in the corner.

"Unless you give a shit what them bitches think, get your butt over here and sit with me." I looked around and seen this pretty blond girl at a table toward the back.

"Are you talkin to me?" I asked.

"Don't let em bother you, honey," she said. "They won't have nothin to do with me either. That horse-faced one over there seen her boyfriend lookin at me and it scared the b'jesus out of her. Now you come in here lookin like you do, with that cute figure, they ain't gonna give you the time of day. You might as well team up with me."

She said her name was Lila. She had two teenage kids and a ex-husband that beat her up one time too many. I told her I was divorced too, and after that first day, me and her got to be real good friends even though we weren't nothin alike. I wasn't used to speakin my mind, and Lila was the opposite. She didn't hold nothin back. If there was somethin she thought needed sayin, she said it. Didn't use polite words either.

22

November 10, 1945 (Sabbath) [Max. 47°, Min. 40°.] High winds all last night, reaching 32 miles per hour, accompanied by a heavy, continuous downpour of rain which lasted all day. I have come to Grants Pass to visit my children and I took them to church. Veda and the children are living in a nice little apartment near her mother. Veda was working, as she has taken a factory job.

RAYMOND TOOK THE TWO older kids to church with him. It was rainin when they got out, but he didn't have sense enough to ask for a ride, so they was soaked by the time they got back. Once Mama got the kids out of their wet clothes and give em some hot cocoa, she let Rosalie take her daddy over to Auntie Bea's house. Bea was givin her piano lessons and Rosalie wanted to show her daddy what she'd learned.

When I got home from work, Raymond was gone and Rosalie was cryin like her heart was broke. Seems she had started playin "Clementine," and her daddy got after her. Told her it wasn't a Christian song and Bea had no business teachin it to her. Not only was she to stop playin it, but she wasn't to go to Bea's house ever again. Rosalie didn't understand what was wrong with a song like "Clementine," and neither did I. She'd been havin fun learnin to play that song, and she wanted to know why God made fun things if people weren't supposed to do em.

Of course I let her go back to Bea's and keep takin lessons. I let the kids do a lot of things Raymond was against. Like singin songs they didn't learn in Sabbath School. Like actin silly, wearin bathin suits, playin in the sprinkler, and chewin gum. He even got after the girls for twirlin around in their dresses, said it was the same as dancin. He'd tell em that those things made Jesus sad, and "You don't want to make Jesus sad, do you?" They was just little kids, for godsake. Good kids. I didn't see a damn thing wrong with em havin fun.

Raymond had plenty to say about me goin to work. Not that he minded me earnin money, 'cause that got him off the hook, but I'd gone and took a job where I had to work on the Sabbath, and that was somethin he never would of done.

And I was wrong about the job not bein harder than takin care of kids. With all that liftin and twistin, I used muscles I didn't know I had. But sore as I was, I felt sorrier for Mama. She was too old to be runnin after four little kids all day long. And to make things worse, my brother Laird had moved back in. He was drinkin real bad and got kicked out of the place he was rentin.

"I can't let him sleep under a bridge, can I?" Mama said. "He'll end up dead if I do."

Laird swore he was done drinkin for good, but then he'd git his paycheck and be gone for two days. Mama'd git frantic and call my sisters' husbands.

They'd find Laird knee-walkin drunk in one of the taverns downtown, or passed out in an alley, and bring him home.

Six o'clock the next mornin, Mama'd start in on him. "Get up, you lazy bum. You're not goin to lay around all day."

"Leave me alone, Ma," he'd say. "I'm sick."

"You're not sick, you're drunk. You're drunk and you stink. Get yourself cleaned up and quit actin like a heathen." She threatened to kick him out, have him committed to a sanitarium, have his paycheck turned over to her so he couldn't git his hands on it. She threatened all sorts of things, but she never did any of em.

So that's why I decided to move into the tool shed behind the house. So the kids wouldn't see their Uncle Laird come home drunk. And they wouldn't hear him and their grandma fight. There was a woodstove in the shed, so I was able to make it warm, and once I got it cleaned up and put our beds out there, it was fine. It was kind of like playin house. Me and the kids, we'd take our baths in Mama's tub, and then go out to the shed and pile into bed together.

But it wasn't a "nice little apartment" like Raymond said. It was a shed. A place to store things. It was full of old Masonite boards and it smelled like turpentine. It was where Laird had always went to paint. He had talent, Laird did. He painted pictures of mountains, lakes, and rivers, with deer and wolves. All so lifelike. He could of made somethin of himself if it weren't for his drinkin. Instead, he just gave his pictures away. Traded em for booze. People said half the bars in Grants Pass had Laird's paintins on the walls.

When Laird was sober he was great to have around.

The kids loved him. He built em kites. Rough-housed with em. Chased em around the yard with a pair of tin snips, sayin he was goin to cut off their ears. They ran and screamed and hid from him, and when he stopped, they begged him to do it again.

Raymond was always writin me letters. Sayin how much he missed his children. Sayin he wished he could visit more often. But he was broke, he said, and couldn't afford bus fare. Then he'd mention havin gone to camp meetin up in Washington State or some other place. It made me mad. I knew what that cost, and it was a lot more than bus fare to Grants Pass. I wondered, though, if the kids weren't better off without him. The longer he was away the less they seemed to miss him. And it wasn't like they didn't have any men around. They had Uncle Laird and Uncle Gabe and Uncle Walt, who all went out of their way to spend time with em.

Walt was my sister Zelda's husband. He was a big, even-tempered, teddy bear of a man. Nothin rattled him. He would take Bubby home with him, keep him overnight. Bubby loved tools and machines and takin things apart, and Uncle Walt would let him putter around in his workshop. But Uncle Gabe preferred the girls. He let them come over anytime they wanted, but he wasn't as patient with Bubby. Bubby got on his nerves. One time Gabe brought Bubby home, pullin him so hard by one ear, the poor kid was clear up on his tiptoes. "Keep this one away from my shop," he said. "He takes things apart and I can't find all the pieces."

23

I WAS EIGHT MONTHS PREGNANT with Sam when I met Ed Landres. It was after my accident and before I'd made up my mind about leavin Raymond. Ed didn't have anythin to do with my decision, but he did make an impression.

I'd just got out of the hospital and was stayin at Mama's house. Mama was takin care of my three kids and I barely left the davenport.

My brother Laird's drinkin had got him kicked out of his place, so he was stayin there too, and that's how I met Ed. He'd come by the house to check up on Laird, and Mama tore into him somethin awful. Far as she was concerned, any friend of Laird's was a no-good drunk, and ever bit as much to blame for Laird's drinkin as he was.

Ed kept comin around, though, even after that tongue-lashin, and I liked how he didn't seem to let Mama git under his skin. He'd set and talk with Laird, and the two of em together put on quite a show, cuttin up the way they did. I got a kick out of watchin him and Laird play with my kids, who loved the attention.

And just seein how much they loved it drove home to me that it wasn't just my life that was dismal, it was their lives too.

It was later, after Sam was born and I was divorced, that I started goin out with Ed. I was workin at the box factory then, and me and the kids had moved into the little shed behind Mama's house, so there was no way to keep her from knowin. She had a conniption fit. Said his kind was no good and if I run around with him I'd end up on skid row with him and Laird and the rest of the drunks.

Ed was tall and blond, with blue eyes and a nice smile. His hair was thin on top, but I thought that added to his good looks. He'd come to pick me up wearin dress pants and cowboy boots, smellin of aftershave. I was a thirty-year-old in what felt like a forty-year-old body, but Ed made me feel young and pretty. And he made me laugh. Lord, it felt good to laugh.

I got myself a couple of new dresses, and when other men looked at me and whistled, Ed didn't mind. Said bein seen with a pretty woman improved his image. He took me places I never been before. Movies, pool halls, and beer joints. I told him I was scared somebody'd recognize me, but he just laughed. Said the folks I was worried about runnin into didn't have no more business bein there than I did.

If there was a jukebox, he'd want me to dance with him. I told him I was raised in a church that taught against dancin and I didn't know how. The only dancin I ever done was with Rheba and Flossie when we were girls, and that was a lot different than dancin with a man.

But the music got to me. Hoagy Carmichael, Johnny Mercer, Cole Porter. I fell as hard for the music as I did for Ed, or at least it was all part of the same thing. That music, bein in Ed's arms, leanin against him, smellin his smell, made me feel things I never felt before. Mama was right about dancin. It could lead to all kinds of trouble.

I loved bein with Ed. The way he kissed me, pressed his body up against me, made me want him like I never wanted anythin. I worried about what Mama would say if I slept with Ed, but I was more worried about God. I had the sin of divorce on my slate already and I didn't want to make it worse.

"Why don't you marry me?" Ed asked after we'd gone out for a while. "Let me take care of you and your kids. Your divorce is final. There's no reason not to."

It was less than a year since my divorce and I knew Mama would be against it, but it was a way out of a terrible situation. It'd be good for Mama, too, in the long run. The little bit of money I made at my job didn't come close to coverin the cost of supportin us. And she was gittin too old to keep runnin after my kids.

Besides, I was fallin in love with the guy. He'd never been married and he liked the idea of a ready-made family. My girls were seven and three, Bubby was almost six, and Sam, my baby, was a year old and just startin to walk. They were all crazy about Ed. When he come to see us, his pockets bulged with lollipops and bubble gum. He took the kids out for ice cream cones, gave em horsey-back rides, and carried the littlest ones around on his shoulders. What could be wrong with marryin a man like that?

24

ED PINNED PINK ROSES on the linen suit I bought with my paycheck. Laird and my friend Lila went with us to be witnesses, and we had a simple weddin in front of a judge. Afterwards, the four of us went out and celebrated.

When we come back to the house and showed Mama my ring, she laid into us like a riled-up rooster. Said it was a sneaky thing to do. I knew she'd be mad. And I didn't blame her. After all, she'd been the one stickin up for me when people talked, defendin my decision to divorce Raymond, takin care of the kids while I worked, and I'd gone off and got married without even tellin her I was goin to. But I wasn't sure what upset her most, us gittin married or me havin liquor on my breath.

Those first weeks, though, I tried to put her anger out of my mind. I was in love. Even my kids took a backseat to Ed and the way my body responded to his touch. I never knew sex could be so wonderful. And there was the time after we made love, when we laid in bed and talked. I'd tell him about my family, and he'd say he couldn't remember his. His dad brought him to Oregon when he was eleven or twelve, then took off and left him with a middle-aged couple named Forester out at Rogue River. They raised him. He didn't recall his mother at all.

He liked to talk about the cabin he was buildin. Said he would take me to see it, but first he wanted to add on another room, put in plumbin, paint it. We agreed I should stay put till it was ready, then he wanted me and the kids to go live there with him. I never got it straight where the cabin was exactly, except it was across the Applegate River. There weren't any roads, he said, so he kept a rowboat out there that he used to git back and forth.

Ed worked for the Forest Service, doin radio repair and watchin for fires. Durin the week he either stayed at the lookout station or at his cabin, and on the weekends, he come back to Grants Pass. He always took the kids and me to do somethin fun, but at night I'd have them sleep over at Mama's.

I quit my job at the box factory and took over the day-to-day care of my kids. Ed was givin me money to buy groceries and pay Mama some rent. That didn't soften her up though. Her mind was made up about Ed and nothin short of him walkin on water was goin to change that.

It never took long for Raymond to git wind of what was goin on in my life, and this time was no different. He wrote to tell me, in no uncertain terms, that by bein "an adulteress" and marryin a second time, I had committed a double offense against God. But what seemed to worry him most was the fact that he was still obligated to send child support. "This new husband of yours," he wrote, "is fully capable of providing for you. And I have it on good authority that he has been using the money I send for my children on tobacco and gambling." In the first place, Raymond almost never sent any money, and whoever told him Ed was usin it for tobacco and gamblin didn't know what they were talkin about.

When I got pregnant, Mama started sayin things like I would of been better off alone with four kids than have five and a drunkard husband. She couldn't see one whit of difference between someone like Ed, who drank a beer once in a while, and a alcoholic like Laird.

Ever'thin Ed did caused Mama to pick on him more. At Christmastime he took the three oldest kids to town to see Santa Claus, and Rosalie talked him into takin em to a movie. She knew enough not to tell her grandma, but Bubby spilled the beans.

"Shame on you," Mama scolded. "You had no call to take them children into a show house. There's no tellin what kind of things was put in their heads."

"Carrie, it was *The Adventures of Rusty*, for God's sake. About a boy and a dog. Where's the harm? They had a good time."

"Just because they had a good time doesn't make it right," Mama said.

The bigger my belly got, the more she grumbled, "Why don't he git you a house? You need your own house. You don't have enough room for four younguns as it is, let alone five."

"He will," I reminded her. "He's fixin up his cabin. You know that."

"Are you even sure it exists? Has he ever taken you out there?"

"No, but he will," I said. "He'll take me when it's ready. When it's nice."

"It's a hare-brained idea, that's what it is." Mama banged a pot down on the stove. "Movin you across a river with a bunch of little children. Plum foolishness, that's what, just plum foolishness."

In spite of Mama's constant naggin about the "sorry mess" I'd got myself into, I was happy. I had my kids, and I had Ed and the weekends to look forward to. Every Friday I made up the bed with clean sheets, took a bath and put on talcum powder. Then I'd git the kids bedded down at Mama's, or at Bea's, and go back to our little love nest, as Ed called it, and wait for him.

He'd come in and scoop me up, and we'd make love. Then he'd throw back the blankets and put his ear on my swollen belly. "Hey baby, can you give your daddy a kick?" When the baby moved, Ed traced the ripples with his fingers. He'd pull me up against him, cup his big hands over my belly, and I'd remember how squeamish Raymond was. How he hadn't wanted to touch me at all.

Ed was so proud when Janie was born. When we took her home, he carried her around in the crook of his arm and talked to her like he expected her to answer him back. She didn't look like my other babies. They all had round faces and dark hair. Janie was long-boned and bald, like her daddy, and he thought the world of her. That was in May. Ed was impatient to finish the cabin and git us moved away from Mama, but to be truthful, I'd got used to the way things were. And hearin Mama go on all week about the foolishness of movin across the river had started to wear on me. Whether I wanted to admit it or not, I was afraid she was right.

Ed took a extra day off over the Fourth of July holiday, and we went downtown to see the parade. It was the first one my kids had been to, and I never seen em more excited. Marchin bands, decorated floats, motorcycles, and fancy cars. The girls strutted like the majorettes, and Bubby run in circles makin motorcycle noises. Then the town mascots, the Cavemen, come along—terrible lookin characters with big teeth and horns, wearin animal skins, and carryin clubs—and started grabbin pretty girls and little kids and puttin em in cages. It was all in fun, but when they got ahold of Bubby, he screamed, and it took me a while to calm him down. But it was a fun day, and bein together like that made me feel like we were a real family.

The summer passed with Ed comin to be with us on weekends and workin on the cabin durin the week. One morning in late November we were in Mama's kitchen and Ed was sayin how close the cabin was to bein done. "I got the plumbing hooked up, and there's just a few more things I have to do before we can move in," he said. "The painting isn't done, but you can help me with that."

"Sure," I said, "I know how to paint."

Mama stopped what she was doin at the sink and turned around real slow. "I've been listenin to you talk about that cabin for months now," she said, "and I've said this before. I think you are out of your mind. Takin five children back and forth in a boat. Little children. They could drown crossin that river. And what if one of em gits sick when you're not around? Or breaks a leg? Or gits snakebit? How would Veda git em to a doctor?"

Ed slammed out the door and I followed him. "Jesus Christ," he said, "doesn't she ever quit?" He didn't stay that night. Said there was some things he had to do. He wanted to git us moved as soon as possible so he wouldn't have to put up with my mama anymore. I was on his side, more or less. He had his reasons for gittin us away from her, but the closer he got to finishin the cabin, the more I worried. Mama had a point. If one of the kids got hurt I'd really be in a fix.

25

January 7, 1948 (Wed.) [Max. 51°, Min. 43°.] Another extremely wet night with rainfall since Monday totaling a little over 4 inches. This is the most rain the Willamette Valley has had in 2 years, leaving me without employment for several weeks.

THE NEXT LETTER I GOT from Raymond was all about the rain where he was and how it was keepin him from gittin any work, which of course meant no child support this month either. He whined about how tough it was findin jobs and how he was not able to even keep a roof over his head. I didn't feel sorry for him. He didn't have to stick with farm labor. He didn't have to work outdoors. Besides, it was rainin in Grants Pass, too, and it wasn't easy for me with the kids inside all day. They were restless. Quarrelsome. That made Mama extra cranky, and on top of ever'thin else I was havin mornin sickness again.

I wasn't sleepin well either. Havin bad dreams. There was one where me and the kids were in a boat in the middle of a river. I was in labor and tryin to git to the hospital. Baby Janie was on my lap and I was tryin to hold onto her and row at the same time. The boat was fillin up with water and I was hollerin at the kids, tellin em to take tin cans and bail. They were all cryin and bailin, but the water kept comin up. Got clear past my ankles. I was rowin and rowin … and I woke up in a cold sweat.

Ed came on Friday, and like usual, the kids slept at Mama's. When we went to git em Saturday mornin, Mama was standin by the door with her coat on, waitin for her ride to church. She started in on Ed. "Listen here," she said. "You need to quit doing whatever it is you do, and stay here. Be a full-time husband. Get Veda a house."

"I'm working on it," Ed said. "The cabin's almost ready. We'll move soon and be out of your hair."

"Phooey. That cabin. It's all I hear from you. Is that your idea of a decent place to live? It's no place to take children and you know it."

"It's not your business." Ed said. "It's between me and Veda. Keep your nose out of it."

"Those are my grandchildren," she said, "and I have every right in the world—"

"Goddammit, Carrie, you've been on my back ever since—"

"Stop it," I yelled. "Stop fightin."

Mama's ride pulled up in the driveway and she slammed out the door. I watched her git in the car, then, before I knew I was goin to, I blurted out about my dream. "It must mean somethin," I said. "Maybe it means we shouldn't move out there."

Ed looked at me. "Jesus, Veda," he said, "I wish you'd told me how you felt before I put all that time and money into the place." He jerked the door open and started to leave.

"Where are you goin?"

"You don't want to live there, fine. I'll go get my tools and board the damn place up. We'll git a house in town, if that's what you want. But it won't be close to your mother."

He walked to his car with me callin after him. "Ed? ... Ed?"

He drove off, and I started to cry. I didn't blame him for bein mad. I should of said somethin sooner. It wasn't fair, springin it on him the way I did.

On Wednesday the headline in the *Courier* said the Applegate River had overflowed its banks. Two people drowned, the article said, and one man was rescued from a cabin out by Murphy. I chewed my fingernails down to the quick, picturin Ed stranded and not able to git across the river. Mama said I was borrowin trouble, that I should wait till he was late comin back before I got all lathered up.

Friday came, and I fixed a nice supper at Mama's. I made biscuits. Ed loved my biscuits. I was all set to tell him how sorry I was, that I'd live anywhere he wanted. It kept gittin later and later, and he didn't come. I fed the kids and put em to bed on Mama's davenport. Then I went out to the shed and walked the floor. It was pitch dark, but I looked out the window ever'time I heard a noise. Around midnight I laid down on the bed, but I couldn't sleep. By mornin I was crazy with worry.

Mama said he was probably too drunk to come home. Bea offered to send her husband Gabe down to 6th Street, where all the taverns were, to look for him, the way he did when Laird went on a bender. I told her no. I knew Ed had to be stranded by the river.

Gabe had worked for the Forest Service and he knew the area, so on Monday him and Laird went to look for Ed. They found his car a ways off the Williams highway near the place where they thought he would have had to cross the river, but the rapids were runnin too fast for em to cross. They got ahold of the state police and were told to give it a few days and see if Ed turned up. Said it was too soon to file a missin person report. "He most likely just run off," one of the officers told Gabe. "It happens all the time. Guy like that, some other man's kids."

The police waited until the water went down, and then did a half-assed search. They found the cabin. His radio equipment was there, and so were his tools. I kept after em, wantin em to do more. "Did you find his boat?" I asked. "You must of found his boat."

"Look, lady," the officer said, "there's pieces of boats strewn all along that river. No tellin who they belong to. Lots of folks out there have boats."

I wasn't stupid. I knew if I come from money, had connections, they would of tried harder. Another week went by and Ed didn't show up. I didn't understand it. Why were his tools there? He wouldn't go off and leave his tools. And why would he leave his car? I cried till I couldn't cry anymore. If it wasn't for Rosalie, my oldest, I don't know what I would of done. She was just nine, but there was times when she took over, seen the kids got fed, told em stories, played games. Kept em busy so they wouldn't ask too many questions.

Ever'body had an opinion. Mama. My sisters. Rheba and Flossie. And of course, Raymond. None of em understood Ed wouldn't just up and leave. They didn't know how he felt about me. Mama was convinced he'd turn up drunk and broke. Said she hoped I had sense enough not to take him back.

Rosalie was the only one on my side. She'd put her arms around me and say, "We know he didn't leave us, don't we?" It's what I wanted to believe. What I had to believe. Thinkin otherwise hurt too much. But questions gnawed at my insides. Were my kids too much for him to handle? Did Mama drive him away? Did I? I was ashamed of not ownin up to my worries long before I did, lettin em build up into one big fear. And I shouldn't of told him about my dream when I did, the way I did. I shouldn't of told him at all.

I couldn't stand the thought of stayin where I was and havin to hear my family talk the way they did about Ed. I needed to get away, to stand on my own feet. I'd depended on Mama for years, and I didn't want to do it anymore. Besides, the memory was too fresh. The bed we made love in. The place he stood makin coffee on our mornins together. The window I looked out of while I waited for him that whole goddamn week.

I hated the idea of goin on relief, but it was better than livin off a poor old woman on a pension. It took guts to walk in that welfare office, to tell em I was a widow with five kids and a baby on the way — the way they looked at me, and how they acted when I said I didn't have a death certificate. Turned out in order to git money to feed my kids, I had to say Ed walked out on me. I hated doin that, but it was either give up my pride or feed my kids, so I said what I had to say.

When I got the first check, I found us a house. It was a terrible place with broken linoleum and a roof that leaked like a sieve, but it was all I could afford. No indoor plumbin either, just a outhouse that smelled so bad I didn't blame the kids for not usin it. I bought a chamber pot, and every mornin I went out, holdin my nose, and emptied it into the hole. And I got a big galvanized tub for our baths.

There was a sawmill behind the house with one a them wigwam sawdust burners. At night I could see sparks shoot out and fall like red-hot rain. I was afraid to sleep. Got a couple of hammers and put em in the windowsills. Showed the kids how to break their way out if the house caught on fire.

I didn't much care if I lived or died. I didn't eat, didn't sleep, and I knew I wasn't doin the baby I was carryin any good. It was Ed's baby and I wanted it, but I was just so sad. I kept thinkin how happy he was when Janie was born, and how he would never git to see this baby. It made me think about the girls whose husbands got killed in the war. How it was for them. But at least they had pictures of em in uniform to remember em by. I didn't even have that.

Eddie was born just thirteen months after Janie. He wasn't pretty like my other babies. His head was shaped like a eggplant and I was told it was 'cause he had rickets. I blamed myself for not eatin right, not takin care of myself. It was probably a miracle he got born at all.

I didn't have enough milk to nurse him, so I had to buy formula. Even then he didn't gain weight the way he should of. He was always catchin cold, too, and so was Janie. They both got bad earaches. I set up nights with em. Rockin. A baby in each arm. If they fell asleep, I dozed off too. Sometimes I'd come back out of a dog-tired half-sleep and see Ed standin there, smilin, holdin a cup of coffee. But it wasn't ever real. He was gone, and I had these two babies that'd never git to know their daddy.

The police said they searched the river. Said if Ed drowned his body would of turned up. I tried to imagine what could of happened to him. Maybe he fell off a cliff. Maybe a animal got him. Or maybe somebody shot him and hid the body. If he had run off, like they said, where would he go? Why would he leave his car? And why would he go off without takin his tools?

Months passed. Eddie gained weight. His head lost its odd shape and sprouted soft yellow fuzz. He was adorable and sweet, and he had Ed's blue eyes. But he still got sick a lot. I tried to keep the house warm, but it was drafty and the electric bill took a big bite out of my welfare check.

The week before Christmas we got our first snowstorm, and I was glad 'cause it give the older kids somethin to be excited about. I bundled em up and watched from the window while they squealed and laughed, and Rosalie showed em how to make snow angels.

The next mornin Rosalie shook me awake. "Mama, come look! Look what the angels brought." On our porch was a big box of groceries. Bread and oatmeal, eggs, canned soup, peaches, Crisco, flour, a sack of oranges, and a dozen cans of Carnation milk. With two babies on bottles, that milk was a lifesaver. There was even a bag of hard candy, the kind with colored stripes, and a Christmas present for each of the kids. I didn't know if it come from one of the churches or some county agency, but if Rosalie wanted to believe it was from the angels, I wasn't goin to tell her any different.

That box of groceries made me think my long string of rotten luck was over, but then Ruthie woke in the middle of the night screamin with a stomach ache. I called my sister Bea, who worked in Dr. Prescott's office. She brought Mama to stay with the other kids, and took Ruthie and me to the emergency room. They said Ruthie had a blockage in her bowel and needed a operation. She was only five years old. I was beside myself, and I didn't know how to git ahold of Raymond. Didn't know if he even had a phone. All I could do was pray.

Dr. Prescott came through the big double doors and pulled off his mask. "She came through just fine. She'll be good as new in no time."

I walked to Ruthie's hospital room on rubbery legs, set down beside the bed, and had a long talk with God. I thanked Him for lookin after my little girl and bringin her through the operation. Then I asked Him real nice if He could please, please, just lay off me for a while.

26

I WAS ALONE FOR MORE than a year with no word about Ed. I missed him, thought about him all the time, and wished he could see his babies. Janie turned two and was startin to talk. Eddie's first birthday was comin up. He was already pullin himself up to things, tryin to walk.

The only friend I had was Lila. She dropped by once in a while, but never stayed long. It was probably a good thing, since she had a mouth like a sailor. She teased me about bein a goody-two-shoes and tried to git me over my Sabbath School upbringin by teachin me to smoke and swear.

"Ya gotta yell at the world when it's pissing you off," she said. "You need to learn to say shit."

"I can't," I told her.

"Yes you can. Come on. Do it. Say SHIT. It won't hurt you."

"No."

"Come on, it feels good. Comm-mahhn, say it."

She got me to laughin, and I said "SHIT" real soft.

"No. Loud! Say it loud. Scream it. Scream SHIT!"

So I did. She was right. It felt good. Damn good.

She was after me, too, to git out and meet people. "You're not doing yourself or those kids any good moping around the way you do. You need to get out and talk to grownups. Christ, I'll bet you ain't had a conversation in months that wasn't about pee-pee or poo-poo."

It wasn't exactly true. I had Rosalie. She was ten and I talked to her. But sometimes I worried I was tellin her too much, makin her grow up too fast. Lila was right. I did need to git out, but even thinkin about it took too much effort.

"Look at yourself," Lila said. "You could pack everything you own in the bags under your eyes. Your hair is greasy and you look like you've been sleepin in your clothes. You're not too damn good to come out and have a beer with me." She said she'd bring her teenage girl to set with my kids.

I liked Lila a lot, but I didn't want to go out with her. I knew what kind of places she went to.

"We can't go in bars," I said.

"Why not?"

"Don't you need to go with a man?"

"Don't worry about that," she said. "I'm fixing you up. The guy I'm seein has a friend. Good lookin guy. Classy dresser. A laugh a minute this one. You'll get a kick out of him."

I took a bath and washed my hair. Then I drug out a dress I hadn't wore since Ed left. When Lila got there, she put lipstick on me and fiddled with my hair. It'd been so long since I fixed myself up, I was surprised how good I looked. We made a odd pair, though, me and her. She was short. I was tall. Her hair was brassy blond and puffed up high. Mine was dark brown and straight. And while she liked squeezin herself into tight sweaters, I dressed like a minister's wife.

The "laugh a minute" was a travelin salesman named Frank that sold ladies' dresses. He drove a big black car with a clothes rack in the back seat, wore expensive lookin suits, and wing tip shoes. He drank scotch, talked fast, and told off-color jokes.

"I told you you'd have a good time, didn't I?" Lila said when her and her friend drove me home. "Frank liked you, wants to see you again. Did he tell you that?"

I hadn't had all that good a time. I felt out a place, didn't git the jokes, or have anythin funny of my own to say. I set there with a fake smile, wishin I was home with my babies. But I agreed to go out with him again 'cause Lila expected me to, and it felt good to git dressed up.

The next time, Frank came to my place to pick me up. The kids, the littlest ones, climbed all over him. He entertained em for a whole hour, showin em magic tricks like pullin nickels out of their ears, before Lila came to take em to her house.

He give me a couple a nice dresses from his car. Had me put one of em on and told me I looked like a million bucks. He'd brought booze with him and asked if I had some glasses. So we started drinkin. He turned on the radio and wanted to dance. I was feelin pretty loose. Missin Ed and likin the way it felt to be in a man's arms again. I let him kiss me.

We had some more to drink. The room spun. His tongue was in my mouth, his hands up under my brassiere. He carried me to the bed and undressed me. I tried to push him off, then gave up and let it happen. He was gone when I woke up. I thought he'd call, but he didn't. I felt sick and ashamed. Empty in a way I never felt empty before.

"What did you think?" Lila said when I told her, "that he'd marry you just because you slept with him?"

"Course not," I said, "but I feel rotten."

"You used a diaphragm didn't you?"

"I don't have one. Why would I?"

"Oh my God, honey, it's to keep you from havin more kids. The last thing you need is another kid."

"Well, it's not goin to happen again."

"Of course it will," she said. "You're a looker. You need to get a diaphragm."

"I can't," I told her. "I wouldn't know how. I'd be too embarrassed to ask."

"Believe me, embarrassed is better than pregnant. I'll go with you. It'll be fine."

Nothin embarrassed Lila. To her, talkin about sex was no different than talkin about cleanin house or cookin supper. She slept with lots of men and she only had two kids. She said I had to wise up and learn how to protect myself. She drove me down to Medford so I could go to a doctor I never been to before. "Don't tell him you don't have a husband," she said when I got out of the car.

The doctor wanted to know if I had discussed it with my husband. Said preventin pregnancy wasn't my decision alone. I told him we had six kids and couldn't afford another baby.

"Still," he said, "I need to hear it from your husband. His wishes have to be considered."

My face felt hot. "I know," I said. "We talked about it. Neither one of us wants another baby."

He dropped his head and looked at me through the top of his bifocals. Then he opened the door a crack. "Nurse," he said, "put her in a room and have her get undressed."

Maybe it was my guilty conscience, but the doctor, his nurse, even the lady at the front desk, seemed to know I was lyin about my husband.

At the car, I waved the prescription in Lila's face. "He made me feel like a criminal."

"What's criminal? Not wanting to get pregnant? What business is it of his?"

"I think he knows I'm not married."

"You *are* married. Remember?"

"Yes, but I don't have a husband, do I? Please, just take me home."

"No. Not until we go to the drugstore," she said. "I know you, Veda. If you don't do it now, you'll never get the diaphragm."

The letter from Mrs. Forester, the woman who raised Ed, came out of the blue. She was widowed and alone, she said, and was writin to ask me to come out to her place so she could see Ed's babies. I'd only met her twice. Once was right after we got married. She wasn't friendly, so Ed never took me back. I didn't want him to. Then when he disappeared, me and Laird went out to ask if she had any idea where he was. I had Janie with me that time, and she could see I was pregnant. She told us Ed stopped comin around. She hadn't seen him in months.

Anyway, gittin that letter made me feel kind of sorry for her. I figured she must miss him too, and maybe I owed her a look at the babies. Lila drove me. The place was out in Rogue River. I remembered that it was way back in the trees and you couldn't see it from the road. We took a couple of wrong turns before we found it. The house was old, wood all weathered and dry, had a big wrap-around porch with a half dozen rockin chairs, all different.

This time she was nice as could be. Oohin and ahhin over the babies, sayin how cute they were, and how they took after Ed. Said Eddie was his spittin image. She didn't ask us in the house, just motioned to the chairs and brought out lemonade. She kept takin the babies, one at a time. Carryin em up and down that long porch, standin at the railin, facin toward the trees. First Janie, then Eddie. Over and over. It give me the oddest feelin. Like maybe Ed was out there. Watchin from behind a tree or somethin. Like maybe Mrs. Forester had got me to come so Ed could see his babies.

Back in the car I asked Lila, "Didn't that seem strange to you? The way she kept doin that with the babies? It was like she was showin em to him."

"What are you talking about?" she asked. "Showing em to who?"

"Ed. I'm talkin about Ed," I said. "What if he was out there? What if he was wantin to see his kids and she was holdin em up for him to see. Showin em off."

"Veda, stop," she said. "Ed's gone. You'll drive yourself crazy thinking he's out there in the woods spying on you."

"But what if? What if he's out there somewhere? Maybe he's in some kind of trouble and he has to hide. Maybe he wants to come back to me. It makes sense that he'd want to see his babies. What if he's still alive and he comes back and finds out I slept with another man?"

"Veda, Ed isn't coming back. You have to accept that and get on with your life."

I tried to git on with my life, but I couldn't stop thinkin

about Ed. I loved him and I wanted him back. But part of me wanted to punish him too. Punish him for leavin me. I let Lila set me up twice after that. "Let em buy you dinner," she said. "Give em what they want. It'll be good for you."

I was miserable both times. I knew what I was doin was wrong. And I worried about what Rosalie knew. She paid attention to things. I wondered what she'd remember when she was older. And what she would think of her mama. I told Lila to stop gittin me dates. I didn't want to go out with nobody.

27

CHRISTMAS CAME AND WENT without hearin from Raymond. He never sent presents, but he did usually send the kids a card. Then in January, I got a letter from him sayin he'd got married.

Said he had been assured by his pastor that he had a "Scriptural right" to do so. That as the "innocent party" in our divorce, he could remarry without damage to either his soul or his standin in the church. His new wife was not Adventist, but he had studied with her, and had her examined by his pastor to insure she was ready for baptism into the Adventist Church. In other words, he made sure she was good enough to marry him.

I couldn't have cared less about him gittin married, but it was another excuse not to send the money he owed me. "I have another family now," he wrote, "which includes two teenage children, and expenses beyond my ability to pay, so I am taking steps to get a legal reduction to my child support."

Well, I had expenses too. The welfare check barely covered the rent and groceries. I was takin in ironin again, doin ever'thin I could to make ends meet. After I put the kids to bed, I'd set up the ironin board, turn on the radio, smoke cigarettes, and stew about Raymond never livin up to his responsibilities. It was one thing to let him slide on child support while Ed was around, but I needed that money now more than ever. The more I thought about it the madder I got. I went back over all the times Raymond fell short. How he'd just accepted the fact that Mama'd feed us, and how he thought my marryin Ed took him off the hook. Now he was tryin to walk away from his obligation altogether.

In spite of the bad feelins I had about the Dorcas ladies takin Raymond's side in the divorce, bein away from the church weighed on me. I had strayed and done things I was ashamed of, and in my mind I could hear Mama ... scoldin, quotin the Bible. And Raymond ... remindin me of my "double offense" against God.

It took me a long time to muster the courage, but one Sabbath I called a cab, and me and my kids marched into church like we never been gone. I got a lot of hard stares that time, but I kept goin. After a couple of weeks folks warmed up, and that was 'cause of Sam. Even self-righteousness melts a bit when a four-year-old wants to shake hands.

The Dorcas Society started sendin over things they thought we could use. There was always baby clothes and things Ruthie and the boys could wear, but almost never anythin for Rosalie. She was startin to fill out, and she was gittin particular about how she looked. If she tried on somethin and didn't like it, she'd do what I used to do, slump and slouch, maybe drag a foot, and whatever it was would look so awful I couldn't bear for her to wear it.

All except for that fur coat. It had belonged to the minister's wife. It looked expensive.

"I'm not wearing that," Rosalie said.

"Yes you are. You don't have a winter coat and this is perfectly good."

"But, Mom, it's ugly."

"No it's not. It's nice," I said. "All women dream of ownin a mink coat."

"But I'm not a woman, I'm a kid."

I made her put it on, and she left for school cryin. I watched her walk down the block, waddlin like a fat little bear, and called her back. I kept her home and we spent all day cuttin my coat down so it would fit her.

It was one thing to give me hand-me-downs for my kids, but the ladies of the church didn't want me anywhere near their husbands. That didn't keep the husbands from wantin to be close to me. I was young and I was pretty. Ed convinced me of that. Not a Sabbath went by that one of em didn't offer to help me with somethin. I turned em all down. All except Charlie Steele.

Charlie was a tall, square-shouldered man who bounced on the balls of his feet like some kind of big shot. And in a way he was. He'd belonged to our church as long as I could remember. He was a deacon, Sabbath School teacher, greeter, usher, collection plate passer, and all around handyman. I knew him and his wife Agnes from way back when I was married to Raymond. Agnes had always been snooty. Held her head so high you could see up her nostrils. God knows what she had to be so proud about. Her and Charlie owned a couple acres with a big garden. They had a cow and some chickens, but the house was shabby.

Didn't even have indoor plumbin. Me and Raymond went there for Sabbath supper a few times. Agnes fed us a good meal, but it was clear she done it out of Christian duty and nothin else.

I almost didn't recognize Charlie. He'd got heavy and lost most of his hair. Combed what he had over the bald place. Still had that proud walk of his though.

I asked about his family, and if they lived in the same place. He said they did. Said their boys were gittin big, and they all kept busy with the garden.

"Say," he said, "we have more beans and tomatoes than we can eat. Could you and your kids use any of it? The extra just goes to waste."

"Well," I said, "since you put it that way, we sure could. That's real nice of you."

"Don't mention it. You'd be doing us a favor." He told me he worked a early shift at the creamery and he'd be glad to drop some things off on his way.

He started comin by a couple times a week and leavin stuff on the steps. He brought eggs too, and gallon jugs of milk. I'd hear him out there settin it down, and after the first few times, I got up to thank him. Ask if he'd like a cup of coffee. Adventists aren't supposed to drink coffee, but Charlie did. He said he wasn't a tight-ass like so many of em. I liked that he could joke like that and still be one.

So that's how it started. Me gittin up and makin him coffee, then settin with him just to talk. Lila had stopped comin around after I told her not to set me up with men, and Rosalie was just about the only one I had to talk to. So Charlie filled a gap in my life. I told him all sorts of things. About why I left Raymond and the hell I went through after Ed disappeared. He was a good listener, and I thought of him as a friend. But I guess he seen it different. After a while he started doin things like pattin my bottom and puttin his hands up under my robe. I told him to quit, that I didn't want him doin it. Said I liked him, but not that way. He'd stop, but then he'd do it again.

"What about your wife," I asked. "What about Agnes?"

He said she wouldn't let him touch her. That she was afraid of gittin pregnant again. I said that wasn't no reason to cheat on her. That she could use somethin, or he could. But he said that wasn't all. He said she was frigid.

"She's still your wife. You shouldn't be messin around with me or anybody." That's what I told him. But the thing was I didn't want him to stop comin to see me. So I went on makin him coffee, and it got to be harder and harder to say no. I let him touch me. Told myself maybe Agnes was cold. Maybe she didn't deserve him. Maybe I did.

Four o'clock in the mornin the kids were asleep. I let him come in my bed, but I made sure he was gone before they woke up. Charlie wasn't handsome and he didn't make me feel the way Ed had, but he was comfortable to be with. I liked how strong he was, and I liked how he smelled. I meant it when I told Lila I didn't want to go out on dates, and I hadn't meant for nothin to happen with Charlie, but it was nice bein with a man again.

28

CHARLIE STARTED SPENDIN more and more time at my place. In the mornin, and then comin by after his shift at the creamery. He was handy at fixin things. Patched the leaky roof, stopped the faucet from drippin, and propped up the place where the porch sagged. He brung over a used bike for the kids, too, and taught em to ride it. Even helped em with schoolwork. They got used to him bein around.

Then somebody reported seein his car parked at my place "for longer than it took to deliver a jug of milk," and the church busybodies swarmed down on us like bees. Three of em come one day, and while one was at the door handin me a casserole, the other two was around the side of the house lookin in the windows. I seen what they was up to and heaved the casserole, dish and all, far as I could throw it. Told em to git the hell outta my yard or I'd call the police. It caused a huge stink. Agnes got wind of what was goin on, threw Charlie out and filed divorce papers.

Charlie found a house on the other side of town, we moved in together, and he started helpin me with the bills. Ever'body was talkin about us and Mama took the news better than I expected. "It's wrong for him to take up with you while he's still married," she said, "but he's a good man and there's not many willing to support a woman with six kids."

In January Raymond wrote that he was comin to visit his children, and I knew it wasn't the children he wanted to see. When he showed up, Bubby and Ruthie kissed him, but Rosalie kept her distance. She still held it against him for sayin she couldn't go to Bea's for piano lessons.

"Happy birthday, darling," he said, handin Rosalie a wrinkled paper sack.

She eyed him, suspicious. He never brought presents. "My birthday's not for two weeks."

The sack held a red plastic pocketbook, the kind you give a three-year-old. Rosalie looked at it and then pushed it up on her arm. The strap was too tight even before it got to her elbow.

"Oh looky, it's a purth," she said, skippin across the floor.

Raymond looked puzzled. "Do you like it?"

"Oh yeth," she said in a little girl voice.

I took her into the kitchen. "That was rude," I said, "you go and apologize."

"But Mom," she said, "I'm not a baby. Why doesn't he know that?"

"It's how he remembers you kids," I said. "Little, like you were then."

"I'll say I'm sorry," she said, "but I don't want his stupid baby purse."

I couldn't let her git away with bein rude, but I didn't like defendin him either. Raymond never did see the kids for who they really were. Didn't notice how they were growin up. Rosalie was almost a young lady.

Raymond hung around for a couple of days, eatin my food and sleepin on my davenport. Charlie stayed away, but if it was proof Raymond came for, he had it. Charlie's flannel robe was on a hook in the bathroom and his shavin mug was by the sink.

"This saddens me, Veda," he said before he left. "I fear for your salvation. And I loathe my children being subjected to this adulterous arrangement."

"You're not sendin me any money," I reminded him. "Maybe if you took care of your kids another man wouldn't have to."

29

March 8, 1951

Dear Sister Landres:
The Church has been made aware that you are living in a
state of sin. Despite the attempts of members to advise you,
you have decided to reject our counsel. We are grieved to
inform you that we will be removing your name from our
membership roll. We continue to pray for your everlasting
soul.

Yours in Christ.

DO YOU SUPPOSE IT was just one self-righteous
sonofabitch wrote that letter," I asked Charlie, "or
did it take a whole goddamn committee?"

"What letter is that?"

"Kickin us outta the church! That letter!"

He give me a blank stare. "I didn't get a letter."

That really pissed me off. They kicked me out, but
didn't do a damn thing to Charlie.

I thought I'd been careful about usin the diaphragm,
but two months went by and I didn't git my period. I

prayed for it to start. Then it got to be three months, and I knew I had to tell Charlie.

He broke out in a sweat. Didn't deny it was his or tell me to git rid of it or nothin like that, but he said it complicated things. Agnes already had a lawyer. She was demandin half his wages and custody of their three boys. He was afraid if she found out I was pregnant, she'd use it to take ever'thin he had.

To keep me from runnin into Agnes or anybody that knew her, Charlie took over payin the bills and doin the shoppin. I didn't mind. I had plenty to keep me busy, and the farther along I got, the less I wanted to go out anyway. It was his idea, too, that when it was time for the baby to be born, we'd go to the hospital in Medford. That way the birth notice wouldn't be in the Grants Pass newspaper.

Our baby girl was born in September 1951. She had Charlie's round face, and she was fat and pink and hungry. When they brought me the birth certificate papers, I looked at the line marked "father's full name" and panicked. I didn't know what to do. Charlie was the father, but we weren't married. How would it look if I wrote Charlie Steele when my name was Veda Landres? So I wrote Edward Landres on that line, even though I believed in my heart he was dead.

We named her Kathy. All the kids were crazy about her, but eight-year-old Ruthie treated her like her very own. Spent hours cooin over her, dressin her, and pushin her up and down the driveway in the old baby buggy we had.

Charlie kept doin most of the errands in town, but when I needed somethin he didn't like to buy, he took me along. I was in the Kotex aisle in the Piggly Wiggly with Kathy on my hip, when I heard someone say, "Is that Charlie's baby?" I jumped, startled. It was Agnes.

I made a beeline for the door, with Agnes hot on my heels, yellin at me, callin me a home wrecker. My heart was hammerin like crazy. I pushed through the door and ran for the car.

Charlie found me there. Said he was lookin for me, didn't know where I'd gone. He wanted to know what was wrong.

"I don't want to live here anymore," I bawled.

"Why? What happened?"

"Agnes happened, that's what happened. Goddamn it, Charlie, I didn't steal you. I tried to tell you to stay with her. I don't want to live in this town anymore. I want to move ... someplace where I can go to the store without bein called a home wrecker. I'm movin... And if you don't want to, I'll go by myself."

Charlie got a job at the Borden Dairy in Central Point, thirty miles south, and told the kids he was goin to work for Elsie the Cow. It was far enough away for my peace of mind, and not too far from my family. Central Point was nothin more'n a few stores and a tall grain elevator. We got a place close to the railroad tracks where ever'body had big weedy yards and vegetable gardens. There was a cobbled together look about the house, different linoleum in all the rooms, doors and kitchen cabinets that, accordin to Charlie, looked like they been salvaged from a army barracks. Charlie and me took the front bedroom and put the baby's crib in with us. We give the girls a room and the boys one, and there was one left over. Could of spread the kids out more if we had extra beds, but they was used to sharin.

Charlie filled the extra room with old radios, record

players, and a big red toolbox full of timepieces. He'd been in the watch repair business years back and it was my guess he didn't remember who any of that stuff belonged to, and their rightful owners'd long since give up on gittin em back.

Movin took a big load off my mind. I felt like somethin broke had got put back together and the church had done me a favor by kickin me out. I planned to eat meat, drink coffee, wear lipstick, and smoke cigarettes right out in the open. And if I felt like havin a drink once in a while, I'd do that too.

Charlie got me a dimestore ring, and I started usin his name. He was good to me and good to the kids. He took us places. Over to the coast, stoppin at all kinds of interestin places along the way, like the House of Myrtle, and those roadside museums where they had dried-up snakes and lizards and such. He took us up to Table Rock so the kids could look for arrowheads, and down to Medford to shop at the Big Y store. The boys especially liked goin to the airport, where we stood by the fence and watched the planes take off and land.

After Charlie's divorce went through, we drove over the state line to Yreka, California. It'd only been four years since Ed disappeared and I didn't think it was legal for us to git married. But Charlie said if we got married in another state, they wouldn't have Oregon records so they wouldn't have no way of knowin.

I started havin that dream again. The one I had over and over after Ed disappeared. I was standin at the edge of a ragin river, trees and boats was goin past, swirlin around, crashin into boulders and breakin up. I could see Ed in the water, goin under, poppin back up, strugglin, flailin with his arms like he was askin for help, but I couldn't hear him callin or nothin. And he didn't sweep past me, downstream, like the other things did. Just stayed in one place where I could see him, fightin the water. I was holdin a baby and I couldn't put her down, so I was runnin back and forth on the riverbank, yellin at him to hold on, to not give up. I'd wake up hollerin, and Charlie'd put his arms around me, ask me what was wrong. I made up things. I didn't want him to know how much Ed was still on my mind.

30

BEFORE, WHEN **RAYMOND** came to see the kids, he slept at Mama's. But since we weren't in Grants Pass anymore, he needed a place to stay. He wrote to ask if I could put him up. It'd been a year and a half since his last visit, so I didn't want to tell him no, but I was nervous about the whole idea. Charlie said it was okay with him, but besides the awkwardness of Raymond sleepin in the same house with me and Charlie, I knew there'd be all sorts of things Raymond wouldn't approve of. It was mid-August and it was hot. I'd been lettin the kids run around in shorts and bathin suits. He wouldn't like that. I'd have to make the girls wear dresses.

"Mom, he's here," Bobby hollered. Raymond stepped up on the porch. He was covered with dust and pantin like he just finished a footrace. He set down his raggedy valise and ruffled Bobby's hair. "Bubby," he said, "Da-dee missed you so much." Bobby ducked. He didn't like anybody messin with his hair and he didn't like bein called Bubby anymore either.

Rosalie stiffened when Raymond put his arms

around her, and even Ruthie, who was always crazy about her daddy, screwed up her face and acted like she didn't want to be kissed. It was little Sam who put his arms out and waited for a hug. Raymond ignored him.

You sonofabitch, I thought, *I'm not goin to let you git away with that.* I shoved Sam in his direction. Raymond looked at him and patted him on the head like he was a neighbor's dog.

"Bobby, take your daddy's bag to your bedroom," I snapped. "You and Sam and Eddie can sleep on the floor in the front room." Rosalie followed me to the kitchen. I filled the skirt of my dress with potatoes, dumped em in the sink and started peelin, skins flyin ever whichaway. "He's got no call to act like that," I fumed, slammin the pot on the stove. "He knows good and well Sam's his." I started slicin a cucumber and cut myself. Blood spurted into the sink and I wrapped my hand in a dishtowel. "Sam looks just like him."

When the potatoes were cooked, I mashed em. I got a jar of string beans from the back porch. Then I sliced some tomatoes and some more cucumbers. "With some bread and butter, that should be plenty," I said. I wasn't goin to put meat on the table and listen to one of Raymond's lectures.

"Why do you always do that, Mom?" Rosalie asked. "We eat meat when he's not here, why are you acting like we don't?"

"I don't know. Just common courtesy I guess."

"Well, I don't think —"

"Rosalie," I said, too annoyed to argue, "go in the other room and visit with your daddy. That's why he's here, to see you kids."

"But he talks to us like we're babies."

"Go on out there."

"And he has hal-i-tosis. Bad."

"Rosalie!"

"Mom, he does. Bad. Can we at least put the bottle of Listerine where he'll see it?"

I gave her a look and she left. I knew she was right about not doin things different just 'cause Raymond was here. It wasn't honest, and I didn't have a good excuse for why I did it.

When Charlie got home, he kissed me on the cheek and went to say hello to Raymond. Charlie'd known him for a long time and always kind of took pity on him. If either of em felt uncomfortable, it was Raymond, not Charlie.

When I had ever'thin ready, I dried my hands, got a Band-Aid for my cut, and peeked into the front room. Sam was holdin his toy airplane over his head makin motor noises. Janie and Eddie were runnin around behind him, and Tippy, the kids' little terrier, was humpin Raymond's leg. Raymond looked like he'd found himself in the middle of a manure pile and couldn't figure a way to git out of it.

I put dinner on the table, and once we all got set down, I asked Raymond to say grace. The kids looked at me like I was off my rocker. We hadn't done grace in a long time.

Raymond bowed his head. "Heavenly Father," he said, "bless this food Veda has prepared to nourish our bodies. Thank you for the opportunity to be here with my children. I ask that you take them in your capable hands and watch over every aspect of their upbringing..."

He took a breath and went on real slow, draggin out his sentences, takin long pauses waitin for the next thought to come to him. I wished I had asked Charlie to do it instead. Raymond stopped to clear his throat.

"...Lord, I thank you for the health of my children ... bestow them with your precious love ... ground their lives in your suffering..."

I opened my eyes and looked around the table. The bigger kids were starin at their dad, Eddie's eyes drooped, and Janie was suckin on the fingers of one hand and twirlin a piece of hair with the other one. I closed my eyes again. *Lord, please let him finish.*

"...Loving Father, in this house where people are estranged from You, enlighten Veda. Show her the sin she is committing by turning these children against the church..."

Bam! Charlie's hand hit the table. "Amen, for Christ's sake. That's enough."

The baby started to cry.

"Let's eat," I whispered. "Food's gittin cold."

We passed the dishes and filled our plates. Raymond leaned over his and started shovelin his food. Rosalie imitated him, turnin her spoon upside down, a habit of his I always hated.

"Stop it right now," I said. Ever'body looked at me, and then got real quiet.

After dinner Raymond brought out a game he called *Bible Authors.* He'd made up cards with quotes, and the kids were supposed to guess what book of the Bible they came from. The kids didn't know the answers, and Raymond didn't hide his disappointment. When Bobby brought out Chinese Checkers, Raymond went to bed.

I could never make sense of my feelins about Raymond. I wondered what I had seen in him. If he really was, once, all that handsome. He seemed so pathetic now. His slumped shoulders, his dour expression, his seedy clothes. But I did feel somethin. Was it guilt? Pity? I couldn't explain it, but bein around him tied my stomach in knots. The next day, before he left, he told me, "I've come to visit because I want my children to see what kind of a man their father is." I think they did. And I don't think it was what he had in mind.

31

THE SUMMER STAYED HOT. Once Raymond was gone, I let the kids run around in bathin suits, go to Saturday matinee movies, and yell and act silly all they wanted to. When school started in September they made friends, and soon we had half a dozen neighbor kids hangin around our house. I loved their energy. I loved the noise.

Rosalie took up with a set of twins from down the street, Marlene and Darlene. I enjoyed foolin around with the three of them. Teachin em songs from the '30s and '40s. Showin em how to jitterbug, Charleston, and cha-cha-cha. We had a good time until the twins started usin bad words around me, and tellin fibs. I scolded em, and they got mouthy.

Things disappeared. My nice cameo pin and a hand mirror Rosalie kept on her dresser. I had my suspicions, but I didn't say anythin. Then Rosalie's favorite sweater turned up missin. It was a present from her Aunt Bea, and I was upset with her for losin it. We searched the whole house and she looked in the lost and found at school. We'd pretty much give up on it, when we run into the twins one day and Marlene was wearin the sweater.

"Where'd you git this?" I asked, pickin at one of the sleeves.

She shrugged her shoulders and tried to go around me.

"I'm askin you where you got it."

"I bought it," she said, "in Medford."

"I don't think so." I pinched the sleeve where I'd fixed a snag in it. "I know good and well it's Rosalie's. Now tell me why you have it."

"Rosalie gave it to me." Marlene glanced at her sister. "Didn't she, Darlene?"

I looked at Rosalie. "Did you?"

"No, Mom, why would I? It's the one Aunt Bea bought for me."

Marlene called Rosalie a name and said she was a liar. She used the f-word, and I lost my temper and slapped her. Told her to bring the sweater back or I'd tell her parents. She brought it back all right. Threw it up on the porch, dirty, and with lipstick smeared on the collar.

A few days later the girls showed up with their dad, who was hoppin mad. He come up to Charlie and started callin him a pervert, sayin he was goin to beat the shit out of him.

"Hey, hold on there," Charlie said, standin up from the lawn chair he was settin on. When the guy seen how big Charlie was, he sort of backed off a bit, but he kept yellin.

"My girls said you been exposing your..."

"Get the hell out of here," Charlie said. He took a step forward and give the guy a shove. "I said get out of here."

"Marlene, Darlene, tell him what you told me. What you said he did."

"He showed us his peter," Marlene spat out. "Didn't he Darlene?" Darlene nodded.

Charlie's face turned purple and the blood vessel on his right temple started pumpin like crazy. He grabbed ahold of the guy. I was afraid he was goin to kill him.

"Stop!" I yelled, pushin at Charlie. "Stop it. I think Marlene's gittin even with me for makin her give back the sweater she stole."

Charlie backed off, his breath raspy.

"What sweater?" The guy croaked, "Marlene? Did you take a sweater?"

"No. Rosalie gave it to me…"

I shook my head. "She took it and lied about it, and I made her give it back."

"Marlene?" He undid his belt and pulled it from his pants. "Tell me the truth. Tell me the truth." He grabbed Marlene by the arm and swung at her with the belt. The two of em went round and round in a circle. Him makin swipes at her, and her screamin and tryin to git out of his way. He was like a wild man. Both girls were cryin and beggin him to stop. Finally Marlene admitted to makin it all up. About Rosalie givin her the sweater and about Charlie showin his peter.

When they were gone, I set on the edge of the porch with my head in my hands. Bile burned the back of my throat. The girls said they lied, that Charlie hadn't done it. But why did they say it in the first place? And why pick on him? Why not say I did somethin? Or Rosalie? My mind reeled. Months back there was talk in the neighborhood about a man. Somethin nasty. I didn't know the details. I wondered if that was what put the idea in their heads. I mentioned it to Charlie, asked him if he had heard anythin. He took it wrong, said I had no cause to question him. Threatened to leave if I thought he was capable of such a thing.

A few days later Charlie told me he had a new job in California. It was so sudden. He hadn't mentioned lookin for a different job. Hadn't said nothin at all. I remembered his face, purple with rage, the night the girls accused him, and how mad he got when I asked if he'd heard anythin. I wondered if somethin else had happened.

"I thought you liked your job," I said. "I thought you liked it here. You said you wanted to stay close to your boys."

Charlie turned his back and didn't answer.

"Does this have anythin to do with them girls?"

"Goddammit, Veda!" he shouted. "Let it go for Christ's sake." He grabbed his keys off the kitchen table and went out the door. I heard the car door slam and gravel spray against the side of the house.

I set down in the rocker with my arms wrapped tight across my stomach. I felt like all the air was knocked out of me. I was scared. Scared I'd blown it. Scared he wouldn't come back. What if he didn't? I had seven kids to raise. How would I support em? I couldn't go back to Grants Pass, not after all that happened, and I didn't have a chance in hell of findin a job. But even worse, what if he really had done what those girls said?

Rosalie come and put her arms around me. "It'll be okay, Mom, don't worry," she said. She went to the kitchen and fixed soup for the kids. Then she got em ready for bed.

It was after eleven when I heard the car. I was still in the same chair, tired but too numb to git up and go to bed. My heart started to race. What would I say to him? What would he say? He come in like nothin was different. Laid some papers on the table and told me he had rented a U-Haul trailer. Said we should start packin up in the mornin. We went to bed, and I kept expectin him to say somethin, but he didn't. My legs ached from tension. I felt cold, and I couldn't sleep.

I pretended to be excited about Charlie's new job. I told the kids it was always sunny and warm in California, that they'd be able to pick oranges right off the trees. They all pitched in to help, and by the end of the day we had ever'thin except the mattresses and a few blankets packed and loaded in the trailer.

We left the next mornin before daylight, and it took me a while to realize we were headed north instead of south. I kept quiet and waited, hopin Charlie was headin up to Grants Pass so we could say goodbye to Mama, but instead, he pulled into one of them auto courts along the Rogue River.

"This'll be okay for a while, don't you think?"

"What do you mean? Aren't you supposed to be startin your new job?"

"Not for two weeks."

"Two weeks," I said, feelin panicky the way I used to when Raymond didn't have work. "What'll we do for money?"

He told me to relax, that he had it under control, but my mind raced on ahead. Why did we leave in such a hurry if he didn't start for two weeks? Why didn't we tell anybody we were goin? Maybe the twins' dad had said somethin to Charlie's boss. Maybe he got fired.

But I couldn't risk askin him, not after the way he blew up last time.

I unpacked a few things from the car, set the baby's playpen up in front of the cabin, and tried to quiet my head. It was November and it was pretty by the river. The weather was perfect. Warm with just a little bit of crispness in the air. The ground was covered with bright orange and red leaves that crackled when you walked on em. I shut my eyes and tried to think about good things. I was in way too deep to rock the boat.

There wasn't much to do. The auto court had a cleanin lady come in ever mornin to make up the beds and sweep the floors. For meals we made do with corn flakes, powdered milk, and baloney sandwiches. Durin the day me and Charlie set on lawn chairs drinkin coffee and watchin cars go by on the highway. The kids loved it there. Janie and Eddie took turns drivin the little pedal car the lady in the office brought over. Ruthie and the boys run around jumpin in piles of leaves and collectin pop bottles to trade at the store up the road for penny candy. Rosalie was too grown up to hunt for bottles, so she just set and read movie magazines and talked the other kids into sharin their candy. When Charlie said it was time to leave, none of us wanted to go.

We left real early again, while it was still dark, and got clear down to Yreka before the sun come up. Ever'thin beyond that point was as new to me as it was to the kids. It all looked so pretty. Mt. Shasta floated up in the clouds like a great big ice cream cone, Lake Shasta's blue-green water was outlined with bright red dirt, and the trees were all dressed up in fall colors. I took a deep breath and blew it out slow.

Charlie looked over at me. "What?"

"Oh nothin," I said. But what I'd done was let go of the heavy weight of trouble I been carryin.

We started seein Burma Shave signs along the side of the road.

To kiss a mug
That's like a cactus
Takes more nerve
Than it does practice
Burma-Shave

The red and white signs were far enough apart so we could read one, then the next, and the next, all of us takin stabs at what the punch line was goin to be.

On curves ahead
Remember sonny
That rabbit's foot
Didn't save the bunny
Burma-Shave

After a stretch there'd be another one.

Doesn't kiss you
Like she useter?
Perhaps she's seen
A smoother rooster!
Burma-Shave

We passed through one town after another. Anderson, Red Bluff, Corning. This part of California, the Central Valley Charlie called it, looked a whole lot different than southern Oregon. No mountains like around Cave Junction and Grants Pass. Just flat country for miles and miles. Lots of tall grass and orchards.

Charlie pulled off the road and stopped. "Look kids, these are olive trees." He climbed out of the car and come back with a handful of olives, gave one to each of the kids. "Go ahead," he said, "try em." While they were spittin and clawin at their tongues, tryin to git the bitter taste out of their mouths, Charlie doubled over laughin. Then he told em olives needed to be cured in lye or salt water before they was fit to eat. His practical joke, comin after a long day squashed together in the back seat, made the kids cranky.

"Stop it."

"You're heavy."

"Mom, make him scoot over."

"She pinched me."

I could tell they were gittin on Charlie's nerves and the last thing I needed was for him to git mad. So I started to sing.

"California here I come, right back where I started from…" I kept it up till ever'body was singin with me, even Charlie.

32

WHEN WE GOT TO WINSLOW where Charlie's new job was, we started lookin for a house to rent. Got a paper and circled all the ads. Soon as people seen how many kids we had, though, they all of a sudden had a policy not to allow children. Or else, the place wasn't for rent after all, even though we had the newspaper ad right in our hands. I was upset, but Charlie wasn't. "Just relax," he said. "Let's look around, see what else is here. We have mattresses and blankets, and if we have to, we can camp out for a few days."

West of town, toward the foothills, we come across a two-story farmhouse settin all by itself in the middle of a field. It looked empty. Me and Charlie went up on the porch and peeked in the windows. There was a few pieces of furniture, a davenport, couple of chairs, but it didn't look like anybody lived there.

"You folks need something?" A man come from around the back, wipin sweat from his forehead with his shirt sleeve.

Charlie told him we were lookin for a house to rent and wondered if this one was vacant.

"Well now, it's vacant alright," he said. "But I haven't thought about renting it. The wife and I just moved out a month ago. Built a new place up closer to the main road. She wanted something smaller. Easier to take care of."

Charlie introduced himself. Said he was here to start work at the creamery in town and needed a place for the family. "Would you consider renting it? We've been looking all day and haven't found anything." He waved his arm out toward the field. "What is that? Wheat?"

"No, it's barley. All of this. By the way, the name's Alvarez," he said. "I'll talk to the wife and let you know tomorrow. Do you have a place to stay tonight?"

Charlie said he'd seen a auto court in town that he thought would do.

"Aw hell," Mr. Alvarez said, "why don't you just go ahead and move in now. Save you a night's lodging fees. I'm sure my wife won't mind."

So we got the house. Mrs. Alvarez come down to meet us, and said if we wanted, we could use the furniture that they'd left.

It felt strange bein in that house with other peoples' things. In one of the rooms, there was a bed all made up with sheets and blankets and a pretty taffeta comforter. There was books, and magazines, and knick-knacks, and a big freezer on the porch that was plugged in and full of food. Wonder Bread, hamburger buns, Twinkies, and those Hostess cupcakes with the white squiggles on top. I made the kids leave it alone, but Charlie laughed at me, said if the owners wanted it, they wouldn't of left it there. I couldn't believe anyone would leave perfectly good food and not be comin back for it. He told me to go and ask, but I never did. It felt too much like beggin.

We'd arrived with enough money to pay rent and turn on the gas and electric, but that was just about all we had. Before Christmas, Charlie got an advance on his pay, so we went out and bought a turkey, some oranges, and a few cheap toys for the kids. Then we drove up to the hills to cut a tree. It didn't feel like Christmas, though. It was way too warm.

In January the kids started goin to the little country school a couple miles from the house. It was two separate little buildins, first through eighth grades, with the kids divided up — Rosalie, Bobby, and Ruthie went to one buildin and Janie and Sam to the other. It was a long walk, specially for Janie, but Charlie mocked em when they complained. Said he'd had to walk twelve miles to school when he was a kid. I didn't believe him and I told him so, but it didn't matter. He said a measly two miles was nothin, and that havin to walk built character. I suppose he was right, but I felt bad for the kids. Janie was just in first grade. Little and skinny, she lagged behind the other kids and they had to wait for her, or go back for her when she tripped and fell down. By the time they got to school, Janie'd usually be muddy or bleedin, her dress'd be ripped, her slip showed, and her socks'd be all the way down in her shoes.

I liked the big old house. The barn. The chickens. That was somethin else the owners left behind, chickens runnin all over the yard, in and out of the barn. They laid eggs any old place. I'd find em and use em, but I had to be careful 'cause they weren't always fresh.

With Charlie at work and the kids at school, I'd be alone with just Eddie and baby Kathy. I felt good about things. I had a husband with a steady job, a roof over my head. I had my own washin machine and a radio. There was a disc jockey on a Sacramento station that I liked, Okie Paul Westmorland. He played country music. I'd put a load of clothes in the washin machine, pick up the baby, and dance all over the house.

On payday, Charlie'd come git me to go grocery shoppin, and on the way home we'd stop for pie and coffee. Just him and me. For a week or so we'd have plenty of food in the house, but by the end of the month we'd be down to beans and cornbread. We weren't goin hungry by any means, but it was hard to come up with things for school lunches that didn't embarrass the kids. They didn't like havin to take a pint jar of beans or a slab of cold cornbread. They wanted sandwiches on regular bread, and treats, like the other kids had. Once in a while I'd git desperate and borrow somethin from the freezer on the porch. I felt bad about it, but I always meant to replace what I took.

That was the year I got bursitis in my shoulder. It hurt so bad I couldn't hardly lift my arm. It made ever'thin hard. Cleanin. Laundry. I had a terrible time liftin the baby. I was in a lot of pain the day of Rosalie's eighth grade graduation, but I wouldn't of missed it for the world. I was so proud of her. She'd already went further in school than I had. I promised myself that all my kids would git the education I never had. Finish high school. Maybe even go to college.

Of the four girls in the graduatin class, my Rosalie was the prettiest. The most developed too. We'd got her a pretty white dress with a gauzy top, so I'd got her a strapless bra to wear with it. After the teacher handed out the diplomas, she asked the sixth and seventh grade boys to come up front. They looked so little standin next to the girls, who had on high-heeled shoes and were as well-developed as any of the mothers in the room.

A square dance record was put on and they all started goin around in circles. Bouncin and *do-si-do-in*, and pretty soon Rosalie's bra started slippin down. Round and round they went with Rosalie *allemande leftin* with one hand and holdin up her bra with the other one. I got tickled and laughed so hard I almost forgot about my bursitis.

The followin week Charlie took me to the doctor and I got a cortisone shot. After a day or two the pain in my shoulder was gone, and I started to git excited about our plans for the Fourth of July. Charlie was gittin three days off, so when we picked up his paycheck, besides groceries, we bought sleepin bags and a whole lot of campin gear.

On the night of the third, we told the kids to git right to sleep 'cause we needed to start out extra early. I put the baby in her crib beside our bed, and me and Charlie stayed up just long enough to git ever'thin boxed up and ready to go.

Charlie was shakin me, yellin somethin I couldn't make out. I tried to open my eyes, but they burned. My chest felt heavy, and a rubbery smell stung my nose. What was he sayin … what? I started to cough. Then I heard a poppin noise and a roar. I finally got my eyes open. Flames. Bright red and orange. The room was filled with smoke.

I started to scream. "Oh my God! Oh my God!" I ran to the crib, "Where's the baby, where's the baby?"

"She's okay," Charlie yelled, "Rosalie's got her.

Come on." He had ahold of me, draggin me toward the door. I pulled away and ran to the stairs. Flames licked the wall. "No," I screamed, "I have to git the kids!"

"They're outside," he said, "they're safe. Come on." He pulled me out the door. The kids were huddled together in the driveway, and Rosalie was holdin the baby. My knees buckled with relief.

"I'm goin back," Charlie said, "The campin gear."

"No," I cried grippin his arm, "leave it." He shook me off.

The house was lit up like Christmas. Huge hunks of wood were breakin off and crashin to the ground. I watched, horrified, as Charlie disappeared in the smoke. It seemed like he was in there forever. Then he came out, empty handed, doubled over and coughin. That's when I realized he was naked. He always slept without a stitch, and he'd been runnin around like that, gittin us all out of the house. I hadn't noticed the fire engines either, till I seen one of the firemen give Charlie a blanket. They weren't even sprayin water. I guess there was no point. The house was too far gone.

I was shakin so bad I was afraid my legs wouldn't hold me up. Someone helped me into the car. I took the baby from Rosalie and hugged the kids. They were all in underwear, I had on a thin nightgown, and Charlie was walkin around in a blanket.

While Mr. Alvarez, the man that owned the house, talked to the firemen, his wife come and crouched down next the car window. She said for us to come to their place. She'd find us some clothes and fix us breakfast. Then, she said, we could figure out what to do next. I reached out and squeezed her hand. I couldn't think of nothin to say.

She found clothes for all of us, even Charlie. Nothin

fit, but at least we were covered. After she fixed us breakfast, she started makin phone calls. I'm not sure who she called or who made the arrangements, but we ended up in that same auto court we'd seen our first night in Winslow. I don't even know who paid for it.

They said it was the wirin that caused the fire. "Old house like that, the wiring just wore out," was what the fireman had told Charlie.

The auto court seemed ever bit as old as the house was and I couldn't stop thinkin about the wires. If I closed my eyes I saw flames behind my eyelids. Thought I smelled somethin. I didn't dare sleep. I got up and checked the stove, the wall sockets, the fuse box, and paced the floor till mornin.

The local newspaper run a story about the fire and about us. Seven children and no insurance. People showed up with things. Clothes and shoes, used dishes, pots and pans. Then the Methodist Church held a party for us in their basement. Cake and punch. Gift-wrapped packages. They give us towels and sheets, blankets, and an envelope with a hundred dollars in it. All this from people who didn't even know us. I was grateful. But I was also ashamed. All the years I was with Raymond, and after Ed turned up missin, I'd had to take charity. I hated worse than poison havin to do it again.

33

CHARLIE WAS ABLE TO find us another house. It was in Alta, a tiny town several miles north. It was a little two-bedroom place with knotty pine walls and a screened-in porch. There was a barn and a chicken coop. Couple of huge trees in the front yard. We'd lost ever'thin, so we spent the hundred dollars at the Salvation Army store on beds, a davenport, and a ice box.

The town had a grade school, but Rosalie would be startin high school, and she'd be ridin the bus into town. I didn't want the kids, Rosalie especially, to start school in other people's hand-me-downs. Charlie told me to stop worryin, that he'd have a couple paychecks before school started and we'd buy clothes then.

None of what we lost had value to anybody else, but losin some of it really hurt. The quilts my mama'd made me, the kids' artwork, and mostly my box of old snapshots, school pictures, and the photos of the kids as babies. Those things couldn't be replaced.

It didn't take long for the kids to git acquainted with the neighbors. Couple of families that lived just one street over had kids about the same ages as mine.

There was a fenced pasture between us and them with a big old billy goat in it. My boys didn't like the idea of havin to go all the way around to see the kids on the other street, so they started cuttin thru the field. Problem was, that goat'd see em and give chase. Well Sam, he was a real fast runner, and he wasn't scared of anythin. So he'd taunt the goat till it started for him and while he was runnin from it, the other kids would make it across the field. It was funny to watch, but I always worried about what would happen if that goat caught up with him. And one day it almost did.

It'd got through the gate somehow and was right on Sam's heels. Sam run in the back door of our house with the goat right behind him, straight through and out the front door. Sam was screamin, and so was I. They went back around house and when Sam run in the back door again, I slammed it. The goat hit the door, and it knocked him stupid. Laid there on the steps for a few minutes, got up, shook his head, and wandered back through the gate. The grade school was just across the field too, so when school started Sam kept on baitin that goat, outrunnin it, so the other kids could take the shortcut.

Rosalie was nervous about startin high school, but with the fire and all that'd happened over the summer, I think all the kids were glad to be goin back to school. On the first day, Bobby and Ruthie brought home papers about rentin instruments so they could be in the band. I liked the idea, but I didn't expect Charlie to go along with it. To my surprise, he did. Took both kids to town and instead of rentin, he bought em horns. Brand new ones, on the installment plan. Ruthie got a cornet and Bobbie got a trombone. For the first few months Charlie made em practice in the barn.

After that, it seemed like Charlie got installment-plan fever. We got us a brand new International Harvester refrigerator. The "femineered" model with the plastic door panels you could change to "match your kitchen décor." Charlie liked the idea of fancy gadgets. The fact that we didn't have a "décor" didn't matter. Then he traded his Buick for a later model Hudson, and again, it was fancy gadgets that sold him. The swivel seat and armrests, the visor over the windshield, the push-button transmission. "Look here," he said, pointin at the buttons on the dashboard. "You could learn to drive it real easy, all you have to do is steer."

He treated door-to-door salesmen like family. Took a likin to the young fellas sellin waterless cookware. There was a easy payment plan, they told us, we could have the "en-tire set for only pennies a day." After the pots and pans, he bought the set of *Encyclopedia Americana* that come with a free bookcase. Then he got the Electrolux.

Salesman come in and threw a bucket of dirt on my clean floor. "Watch this," he said, turnin on the bullet-shaped silver and red machine and suckin the dirt up.

"Yeah, that's nice," I said, "but we don't need a vacuum cleaner. We don't have any rugs."

That didn't faze him. "You got beds, right?"

Charlie took him in our bedroom and pulled back the sheets. When he seen how much dirt come out from one little corner of the mattress, Charlie shook his head. "Well I'll be," he said. "Where do I sign?"

Ever'time one of them slicky-haired doorknockers started workin on Charlie, I sweated. He'd buy things, then the easy payments piled up and he was never around to deal with the bill collectors. He'd tell me to put em off, to say we'd catch up next month. But we didn't. The men that come to take things back—the encyclopedias, the pots and panse, the Electrolux—weren't near as friendly as the guys that'd sold em to us.

After that Charlie got it in his head we needed a television set, and since we didn't have all those installment payments anymore, we could afford it. So a brand new Emerson TV came to live in our house. It was brought by a short fella with a gimpy leg who then climbed up on our roof with a metal contraption he said was needed to git a picture. While he was on the roof, Charlie was in the house hollerin at him out the window. "There. No, not there. Back just a bit, that's better. Now. No, back some more." The picture and sound faded in and out, hissed, got snowy, clear, then snowy again. This went on for a long time till finally Charlie yelled, "Okay, that's it, okay."

When the kids come home from school, Pinky Lee was dancin across the screen. For the rest of the day we all set in front of the television set, watchin *Howdy Doody*, *The Soupy Sales Show*, and *The Mickey Mouse Club*.

For all I know, ours was the first TV set in town. Every kid in the neighborhood was at our place. Sprawled on the furniture, on the floor, or with their noses pressed against the window if I'd just mopped the floor and made em stay out.

It was on all the time. When the daytime shows went off, there was the nighttime ones. Milton Berle, Ted Mack's *Amateur Hour*, *Your Show of Shows* with Sid Caesar and Imogene Coca. We watched till the only thing on was the test pattern, and we even stared at that till it went off the air.

When the Reverend and Mrs. Bergstrom come by one night to invite us to visit the Lutheran Church, they stayed so long I suspected seein the television set was their real reason for comin by. I agreed to go, though, 'cause I hadn't been to church in a long time, and I wanted to show the Lord how grateful I was for sparin us from the fire. I went two more times after that, but the Lutheran service didn't feel right to me. It was just too different from what I was used to.

34

DADDY SHOWED UP at my school, Mom." Rosalie slammed the door and threw her books on the table. "At my school! Gawd. In that old blue suit of his, the one with the pant legs four inches above his shoes. A suitcase in one hand and a Bible in the other. Why didn't you tell me he was coming?"

I hadn't told the kids about his letter 'cause I didn't think he'd actually show up. It was a long ways, and I thought he'd find out how much the bus ticket cost and change his mind. That's what I was hopin anyway. After all this time, I still broke out in a sweat at the thought of seein him. Besides, he should've had enough sense to go to the creamery and wait for Charlie to git off work, not show up at the high school.

All afternoon I made the kids leave the television off so they could visit with Raymond, but like all the other times, he talked to em like they were babies and he didn't act interested in what they liked to do or what they were learnin in school. I wanted him to see how smart they were, to recognize that they were growin up.

"Rosalie," I said, "show your daddy that report you got a A+ on." She made a face, but got up to find it.

"Sam," I said, "go git that model car you built. Ruthie and Bobby, git your horns. Play your daddy one of the pieces you learned in band."

Rosalie and Sam got half-hearted praise. But the Souza march Ruthie and Bobby played wasn't much to Raymond's likin. He preferred hymns, he said. He wished they had taken up the organ instead. The organ? Finally I said, "Why don't you all go outside? Show your dad the animals you're raisin for 4-H."

When I seen Raymond comin back toward the house pickin at his shoe with a stick, I had to laugh. He'd stepped in chicken shit, and it served him right. After supper, it was me that turned the TV on. I didn't care if he was offended. He turned away and buried his nose in his Bible, and if he had any thoughts about lecturin us on the evils of television, he probably didn't dare after the way Charlie stopped him mid-prayer the last time he visited.

Charlie always looked better to me after Raymond had been there. Charlie paid attention to the kids, let em be kids, took em places. We were all a lot better off. But Charlie had his faults too. Even though he held down a job, he was careless about money. He'd cash his paycheck, take me to buy groceries, and pocket the rest. Then when it came to payin the bills, there'd never be enough to cover what we owed. Things got put off. The doctor. The phone bill. The rent. We were late three months in a row so I didn't blame the landlord for wantin us out, but Charlie did. He said we were payin too much in the first place, and he knew of a house in Winslow we could git for less.

35

THE KIDS LOVED BEIN right in town. They could walk to the swimmin pool, stores, and the movie theater. And that gave em reasons to earn spendin money. Rosalie got a job at the local soda fountain, Bobby got a paper route, Sam lined up lawnmowin jobs, and Ruthie cleaned house for some neighbors. Even Janie and Eddie got pennies and nickels from collectin pop bottles. I was the only one without money of my own, and when we run out of bread or milk, or if I needed cigarettes, I had to borrow from the kids.

Charlie was fine with em earnin money, but he didn't like em havin so much freedom. He got more and more crabby. He didn't like the kids runnin all over town. Didn't like the looks of their friends. Juvenile delinquents, he called em, like ones he seen on TV. But it wasn't just on television, he claimed. He'd seen em in Winslow. Hoodlums on street corners, wearin Levis and black leather jackets, cigarettes rolled up in the sleeves of their tee shirts. Seen em drag racin, drivin to the edge of town and back with their radios blarin that rock and roll music, honkin their horns, and yellin things at each other. Lookin for trouble.

Even if Charlie had seen them things, it didn't have nothin to do with our kids. Not a one of em had give us trouble, unless you counted Bobby and that friend of his takin my Pall Malls and smokin em. They only done it once, 'cause when I found out, I made em smoke a whole cigarette with their hands behind their backs. Turned em green as bottle glass.

Still, Charlie didn't like the kids Rosalie run around with. And he thought Bobby bein quiet meant he was up to no good. He didn't like Ruthie listenin to that Presley fellow either. He wanted the kids to have animals to feed, like when we lived in Alta, and he wanted a garden. Said the only way to keep kids out of trouble was to move out of town.

So he took to drivin the county roads. Found a vacant house he thought we might be able to git cheap. It took him a month to track down the owner, a man named Harmon. Besides the house, there was a barn, chicken coops, and a couple acres of weeds. Charlie called it the "Harmon Ranch."

We moved when school let out in June. None of the kids were happy about it. And neither was I. Six miles out of town might as well of been a hundred. Come September all the kids would be in school and Charlie'd be workin. I didn't drive, so I'd be stranded.

Charlie promised Rosalie she could keep her job in town if she'd walk to the creamery when she got off work, and ride home with him. He said he'd take Ruthie in to town so she could play with the band at football games, but she had to give up the idea of goin to the dances and such. That'd mean too many trips back and forth and she'd have plenty of chores to keep her busy anyway.

I hated the house. The broken linoleum, the rusted kitchen sink, the shit-brown walls. I wondered if there was anythin I could do to make it livable.

For the first week I scrubbed floors, windows, walls, and tried to talk Charlie into paintin over that awful brown. "The house can wait," he said. "We need to get the garden in."

"It's too late," I said. "It should've been started months ago to do any good."

He went ahead anyhow. Made the boys turn up the dirt. Then give us all packets of seeds and told us where he wanted em to go. By the time the seeds sprouted it was July and over a hundred degrees. The soil caked and cracked in the sun, the plants wilted, and weeds took over. Charlie made the boys stay outside and hoe the weeds while he set in the house in front of the swamp cooler.

And the animals. First Charlie bought an old cow. Then he got some baby chicks and a pair of rabbits from the Co-op. He handed out chores the same way he did the seed packets. Bobby was to take care of the chickens, Sam was to weed the garden, and he put Eddie in charge of the rabbits. The girls' job was to help with housework, and since I was the only one except Charlie that'd ever milked a cow, that job was mine. I sort of liked milkin the cow though. She was gentle, and there was somethin comfortin about restin my head against her warm flanks, the musty smell of the barn, and the ringin sound the milk made when it hit the pail.

I doubt Charlie knew it when he took the place, but the "Harmon Ranch" was surrounded on all sides by rice fields. And there's no place better for breedin mosquitos than a flooded rice field. All summer long, me and the kids were covered with bites that swole up like goose eggs, but Charlie never seemed to git bit. Mosquitoes weren't the only pests we had. Flies, crickets, no-see-ums, ants. In the evenin, soon as we turned lights on, there'd be moths and mosquitos circlin the light bulbs, buzzin our ears, and landin in our food while we ate supper. And I was always findin black widow spiders near my washin machine.

The heat was almost unbearable. But even with the heat and mosquitos, I liked summer best. That's when the kids were around. The rest of the year I was alone all day in that awful, lifeless house.

Every year Charlie demanded more of the boys. He got more chickens for Bobby to take care of. He got turkeys, too, and the rabbits multiplied. It was Eddie's job to feed the rabbits. He'd go out in the mornin before school and pull grass to put in the cages, but by the time Charlie went to look, the rabbits had eat it all. Charlie never believed Eddie fed em, and Eddie would take a whippin rather than say he hadn't. I should have stood up to Charlie for bein so hard on Eddie, and I tried, but whenever I said somethin, he'd git really mad. And I hated the turkeys. We all did. They'd hang around the kitchen door, shit all over the steps, and ever'time any of us went out, they'd flog us with their wings and peck our legs. I had varicose veins, and I was afraid if they pecked me in just the right place, I could bleed to death. The only way to back em off was to hit em with a stick or a broom, and Charlie didn't like us doin that 'cause it bruised the meat. When it come time to kill one of them cussed birds for Thanksgivin or Christmas dinner, I didn't feel bad about it at all.

36

BUT SOMETIMES **CHARLIE COULD** be a lot of fun. We'd go campin, swimmin in the river, or over to Chico to Bidwell Park. We played games, Monopoly, checkers, cards. Charlie liked recitin poems, and challengin the kids to memorize em. He liked to cook, and the things he made were mostly good. Except for his pancakes. He always managed to burn em on the outside, but they'd be raw in the middle and heavy as a dinner plate.

And he helped the kids with their homework. The problem with that was he thought he was smarter than ever'body else. If he didn't agree with how they were told to do somethin, or if he thought their textbooks had somethin wrong, there'd be a big argument. And it didn't help to tell the kids their teacher "didn't know his ass from his elbow."

And as time went on, he got stingy. Complained about the cost of laundry soap, shampoo, toothpaste. Jumped on us for usin too much hot water or too much toilet paper. He'd check the electric meter to see if the little wheel was goin around and, if it was, he'd go through the house lookin for the culprit. A light that was left on, a radio, a cord that was plugged in, lettin the juice leak out and wastin money. Then he'd go buy some silly appliance we didn't need. Bought one of them things you make labels with and pasted his name on things. Like he had anythin worth stealin. One day he came home with a Osterizer.

"What is it?" I asked.

"It's a blender," he said. He set it on the kitchen counter and plugged it in. "Watch this." He cracked a couple eggs into it, added vinegar and salt, and pushed a button. It made a awful racket and churned while he poured salad oil through the openin in the top. In seconds the mixture got white and creamy.

"Mayonnaise!" he said, lookin proud of himself.

"Wow," Rosalie said, "if we make all our own mayonnaise, maybe we can afford to buy toilet paper."

He didn't say nothin right then, but I knew he'd stew over Rosalie's remark and wake me up in the middle of the night to tell me he was tired of her sass. Say she had a smart mouth and it was my fault for lettin her get away with it. Once he got started, he'd go on for hours. She went too many places, he'd say. He didn't like the boys she went out with. She stayed at her girlfriends' houses too much, and she didn't help enough around the house. I'd tell him she helped me plenty and that she hadn't gone anyplace in months. I'd beg him to let me sleep, but I'd be so tense by then, I couldn't.

He did that any time one of the kids did somethin he didn't like. Any of em except Kathy. She was the baby. He never got upset with Kathy.

By then the TV had become old news. Charlie didn't want the kids watchin it so much. He said it was makin em lazy. They needed to be outside, doin chores, gittin exercise. I did let em watch some shows, though, like *American Bandstand* that come on right about the time they got home from school, but I made sure the TV was off when Charlie got home. Then he would turn it on and watch what he liked—boxin matches, Arthur Godfrey, George Gobel, Lawrence Welk. He loved Lawrence Welk.

Charlie said the kids didn't do enough to help me. But they did. In ways he didn't understand. They entertained me. Made me laugh. We laughed a lot, and it was laughter that kept me goin.

Rosalie was a natural storyteller. A comic. She'd sing, "Bringin in the Sheets, Bringin in the Sheets, We will come rejoicin, Bringin in the Sheets..." while we took the laundry off the line. She'd put underpants on her head and throw socks while we folded clothes. She'd waddle around the kitchen pretendin to be Agnes Gooch from the *Auntie Mame* movie sayin, "I lived, I lived," or squeak like Prissy the maid in *Gone with the Wind*, "Miss Scarlett, I don't know nuthin 'bout birthin no babies."

I was hangin up the wash and she was tellin me about her date the night before. "So he drives to this place and parks," she says, handin me one end of a bed sheet. "He thinks I'm going to make out with him, but I've already decided he's a creep. He slides the seat back and turns on the radio. So smooth. Then he takes his jacket off. And you know what he does? He reaches in the glove box and gets out a jar of Vicks..."

I pick up another sheet, pin it to the line. "I'm listenin."

"…and he starts puttin it in his nose." She screws her finger around inside a nostril, and I start to laugh.

"Can you imagine, Mom? Gawd, he wants me to make out with him and he puts Vicks up his nose?"

I didn't like her bein in parked cars with boys, but here she was tellin me about it, actin it out, and makin me laugh, so how could I git mad at her. She still hadn't done a lick of work, but watchin her and laughin with her was worth a lot more than havin her hang up the wash.

Sam was funny, too. And he was musical. There was a old piano in the house and he taught himself to play it. We all liked to sing. I taught the kids songs I learned when I was a girl, and they taught me ones they heard on the radio. I had a lot of fun singin and cuttin up with my kids.

There was other times, though, that they made me so mad I felt like stranglin em. Charlie said I was gullible and the kids took advantage of that. They played tricks on me and laughed at me when I did somethin dumb. Corrected me all the time, too, just like Raymond did.

"It's *sit*, Mom, not *set*. You're supposed to say *I saw it*, not *I seen it*. Chickens *lay* eggs, people *lie* down."

"It don't make no difference," I'd say. "You know what I mean." The madder I got, the harder they laughed. One time when we were shoppin, I got tired and told em I'd meet em at the car. When they found me settin in a Ford half a block from where our Buick was, they acted like it was the stupidest mistake in the world.

"Well dammit," I said, "it looks the same. It's green. I thought it was ours."

They thought I was hilarious. Especially when I

embarrassed myself. Like the time I run out of a store 'cause the clerk was a man and I didn't want to ask him where to find the Kotex, or that time the elastic broke on my underpants and I had to walk around all day holdin em up through my dress. The one they thought was funniest, though, was the time I got my bra strap caught on the car door handle. I was wearin a sleeveless blouse and my bra strap had slipped down on my shoulder, so when I bent down to put somethin through the car window, the strap got caught. I got in the car, worked my arm out of the blouse, and unhooked my bra from the back. It come loose and slingshotted out the window. Hit an old man standin on the sidewalk.

But teasin me or not, I loved havin my kids around. It was the isolation that made those years on the ranch so hard. I had no friends. No hobbies. The kids were in school all day and Charlie barely talked to me when he was home. I tried to keep things up. Fix meals. Take care of the animals, the garden. But more and more I didn't feel like doin any of it. Dishes didn't git washed. Laundry piled up. I couldn't face the ironin. I was tired. Wore out. And I was sad.

The kids were growin up way too fast. Rosalie and Ruthie had turned into young ladies. Bobby had gotten tall. He reminded me of my brother Laird. Same skinny frame. Same thick reddish brown hair, same deep set eyes. And Sam, my athlete, had his heart set on bein a football player. He was short and skinny, but determined. He sent away for some Charles Atlas exercise books, got a big iron bar from someplace and built a set of weights with old tires, rims, and cement blocks. Went around flexin his muscles. Sayin, "Feel this. See how strong I am."

Rosalie and Bobby got their driver's licenses and Charlie bought a old Plymouth for em to use. It made me nervous, havin em out on the roads. Specially at night. There was no streetlights on those county roads, and in the fall and winter there was a thick ground fog called "tule fog" that made it nearly impossible to see. It was known to cause a lot of car wrecks, and it worried me.

37

WE SET IN THE GRANDSTAND at the football field and watched Rosalie walk with her senior class. My throat ached with pride and somethin else I couldn't quite name. Emptiness maybe. She was the first one of my kids to finish school, and it was just a matter of time before they all would. They'd be leavin home one by one. I didn't know how I'd git along without em.

After graduation Rosalie went to workin full time at the soda fountain. She thought she'd earned the right to be treated like a grownup, but Charlie didn't agree. He kept treatin her like a kid and when he didn't like what she did or who she was with, he'd take his anger out on me. When she was out at night, he'd walk the floor, yellin at me about her attitude. She didn't respect him. She was runnin wild. She was goin to git herself knocked up. I'd lay in bed pretendin to sleep, prayin he'd stop, tension risin off me like heat off a sidewalk.

Charlie found fault with all her boyfriends until she started datin Pete. Charlie liked him. We all did. Home on leave from the Air Force, Pete was polite and intelligent. Good lookin too. I watched him and Rosalie with somethin like envy. The way he looked at her, and how she was so protective of him. He give her a ring at Christmas, and they set the date for the end of February. I was almost as excited as she was.

I never liked February, but havin the weddin to look forward to lifted me out of its grayness for a time. Rosalie made decisions about invitations, flowers, and cake, while me and Ruthie sewed bridesmaid dresses. All the plannin made me remember how hopeful I was about my own weddin. And how disappointin it had been. The yellow dress. The weddin night at my folks' house. The divorce. Things would be different for Rosalie and Pete. I just knew it.

And the weddin was perfect. Rosalie was beautiful. The bridesmaids pretty in their red dresses. And Kathy, my baby, already eight years old, so cute and serious walkin down the aisle with the basket of rose petals. Afterwards, in the church basement, Pete's buddies made toasts and told stories on him while we had cake and punch. Charlie took pictures with his new Kodak camera. And when the bride and groom drove away, I bawled my head off.

With Rosalie gone, the gray returned. Fog rolled in and set on the ground for days. It turned cold, the kind of cold that creeps in and hangs on, damp, like wet wool. But it wasn't just the cold and the fog, somethin else gray and heavy took hold of me, weighed me down. A sadness. A sickness of spirit. I missed Rosalie. I needed her to prop me up and make me laugh.

My head ached. My back ached. I was face to face with that awful brown livin room we never got around to paintin, Charlie's old recliner that spit out hunks of foam-rubber whenever he plopped down in it, cigar butt-filled ashtrays, and a sink full of dirty dishes. Just seein all that made me so tired I'd go back to bed and stay there.

The days ran together. I'd hear Charlie leave for work, hollerin at the kids to git up. I'd hear cupboard doors open and close. Arguments. Ruthie makin lunches, helpin the little kids look for shoes, books, homework. Hear her gittin milk money outta my purse. I'd fall back asleep.

Then I'd hear em come home. Droppin books. Openin the refrigerator. I'd look at the clock and think, *Oh shit, I've done it again*. I knew how much they hated comin home to a dark, cold house with breakfast dishes still on the table, oatmeal stuck to the bowls. I hated it too. I hated the kind a mother I'd become. I'd drag myself out of bed. Go to the kitchen, tell em I was sorry, and start supper.

There was some days, though, when I felt better. When I got up and combed my hair, put on lipstick. I'd mop floors, clean closets, take down curtains, and scrub walls. The kids'd come home and find things upended and the house smellin like Lysol. They didn't know what to make of me on those days. But I knew it made em happy.

Rosalie's husband got out of the service and took a job in Redding. When they told me Rosalie was expectin a baby, I couldn't of been more pleased. I got out my sewin machine and spent the next few months makin flannel nighties and baby blankets. And when Pete called to say they had a seven pound, six ounce baby girl, I packed a bag and went up to Redding on the bus.

Baby Sarah was almost as beautiful as her mama had been. I watched Rosalie hold her and nurse her, rememberin how much I loved doin that for my own babies. I left after a week, full of pride, and knowin it was time to let Rosalie and Pete be alone with their baby.

38

BOBBY JOINED THE AIR FORCE and left for basic trainin the summer after he graduated, and even though he was the quietest of my kids, I felt his absence. Then Ruthie's boyfriend, Mike, joined the Navy and when he came home at Christmas, he bought her a ring. She was still in school and he was bein sent overseas, so they didn't set a date, but I knew it wouldn't be long before I lost her too.

Sam had started high school. He wanted to play football, but Charlie wouldn't let me sign the permission slips. The insurance cost too much and there'd be too many trips back and forth to town. He said he doubted Sam would make the team anyway. I thought Charlie was way too harsh. Always sayin things like that. Tellin em they wasn't good enough. Sam had been hopin to play football for such long time. It just wasn't fair.

That spring Mr. Harmon told us he wanted the ranch back. No hard feelins, but his son had got married and needed a place to live. We moved back to town and this time we got a nice house. It was fairly new with light colored walls and big windows that let sunlight in. It was so bright and nice that even our old furniture looked better. There was a lawn, and a lilac tree outside the front door, and bein there made me feel like a whole different person.

And then Rosalie's husband changed jobs. They moved back to Winslow and rented a little house right across the street from us. I was happier than any time I could remember. Baby Sarah was startin to walk and talk, and Rosalie was pregnant again. This time with twins. It couldn't of been more perfect.

But things never stayed perfect, not in my life anyhow. Charlie got told the creamery was closin. He'd either have to transfer to a plant farther south or be out of a job. Leavin Rosalie and the babies was like havin to cut off one of my own arms. For days I wallowed in self-pity. I needed Rosalie, needed the babies. I was sick of movin and sick of not havin roots.

"It's not that far," Charlie said. "Less than two hundred miles. We'll come back to visit." But I knew it wouldn't be like that. We'd visit at first, but then Charlie'd git tired of the drive and wouldn't want to do it anymore. I was angry and I wanted to blame somebody. I wanted to blame Charlie. But the plant was closin. I couldn't fault him for that.

Ruthie had graduated and had job, so she decided to move in with Rosalie and Pete. The four younger kids, Sam, Janie, Eddie, and Kathy would go with us, of course. Since we'd moved back to town, Sam had finally got his chance to play football, and Janie'd got on the cheerleadin squad. I hated havin to uproot em.

Charlie drove down alone to find us a house. I told him

it didn't matter to me what he got. I wouldn't have Rosalie. I wouldn't have my grandbabies.

What he did git, though, was nicer than what we could afford, and he had no business takin it. The rental agent was his new boss's wife, and he didn't want her to think he was cheap. After payin for the U-Haul truck, the cleanin deposit, and all the hook-up fees, we had to borrow from the kids to buy groceries and gas. Sam got hit hardest. He'd spent the whole summer before we moved haulin hay, and he'd saved up close to five hundred dollars. He planned to buy a car soon as he turned sixteen. I felt sick ever'time Charlie asked him for a loan. I knew he wouldn't git it back, and Sam knew it too. I seen it in his face.

It took me a long time to meet any of the neighbors. We'd see cars on our street, but ever'body came and went through their garages. The kids made friends at school and Sam got on the football team, but Charlie wouldn't spring for contact lenses, so Sam spent most of the season warmin the bench. But in the spring he started runnin track. He was good at that. Real good. He'd always been a fast runner, ever since he was little.

39

"I T'S LONG DISTANCE," Charlie said, handin me the phone. "It's your sister Bea." My heart sank. She almost never called unless somethin was wrong.

"Mama fell and broke her hip," Bea said.

"Oh my God, is she—"

"She'll be fine. She's in the hospital, but she'll need someone to stay with her when she gets out. I can't because of my job. Can you come?"

"Of course I'll come. I can help git her settled someplace, but I can't stay. I have a family to take care of."

"That won't ... Veda, she says she won't go to a nursing home. Can you take her? You know, to live with you?"

I hesitated. "We don't have room, Bea. Our place is small, and I still have four kids at home."

"I know, but I have an idea," she said. "Why don't you and Charlie look for a bigger place? One with a mother-in-law apartment."

I looked around for Charlie, but he'd went outside.

"We can't afford—"

"Listen," Bea went on, "we would all help scrape together a down payment. I have some money, and Wilbert has the settlement from his accident. We've talked about it, and the others say they'll pitch in too."

"I don't know, Bea."

"You're her favorite, Veda, you always were. Think of all the times she took you and your kids in and gave you a place to live. Fed you when you didn't have any money. What do you say?"

I didn't need her to tell me how much I owed Mama. I knew that. And I wanted to help. But have her live with us? I didn't know how that would work.

"I don't know." I said again. "It's not just up to me. I have to talk to Charlie."

For two days I put off bringin it up, but the more I thought about it, the better it sounded. If we bought a house, we'd be set. We wouldn't be throwin money away on rent for the rest of our lives. And Mama would be company for me. Finally, when I screwed up my nerve and asked Charlie, he jumped on the idea. Said he knew of a place that was just the ticket. With a separate apartment like Bea talked about. Said it was kind of run down but could be nice if it was fixed up. Mama'd be able have her own kitchen and bathroom, and I'd be right there close if she needed me.

I went up to Grants Pass on the bus. The medication Mama was on made her groggy, and when it wore off, she was in a lot of pain. She needed help with ever'thin. Charlie went ahead with the business of buyin the house, so after a couple weeks I needed to git back to sign the papers. My sisters agreed to take turns bein with Mama till she was well enough to travel.

While we waited for the sale to close, I started to git

cold feet. Havin Mama live with us sounded like a good idea when I talked Charlie into it, but after bein up there in Oregon with her, and seein how much help she needed, I was startin to have doubts. Besides, I'd forgot how hard she was to be around. Much as I loved her, we hadn't always got along. She had strong opinions. Sometimes she sounded just like Raymond, and I had never learned to stand up to her.

The house was a long step down from the one we'd been rentin, but I liked knowin it was ours. We painted the rooms where Mama would be. Put up curtains, rented a hospital bed, built a ramp up to the porch, and installed grab bars in the bathroom.

Mama's doctor in Oregon said she could travel if we took it slow. We drove up to git her, and on the way back, instead of hightailin it straight through the way Charlie did when it was just me and the kids, we had to stop every night. It took us three whole days, with Charlie in a black mood, Mama moanin ever'time we hit a bump, and me tight as a piano wire tryin to keep peace. Then, once we got home and got Mama settled in, Charlie complained about the extra expense. Especially the sky high electric bills that come from Mama wantin her rooms kept at eighty degrees all the time.

Takin care of her was even harder than I thought. She couldn't do anythin on her own. Go to the toilet, git dressed, move from the bed to a chair and back again. And I knew if I complained about how much work she was, it'd just add fuel to Charlie's fire.

On top of all the work, Mama wanted my company all the time. Whenever I went to do things in my part of the house, she called me to come back. Wanted me to git this thing or that thing, read the Bible to her, turn on the television, or just set with her and listen to her talk.

It pained her that I'd left the church, and she was always leanin on me about goin back. I might of done it, too, if I hadn't been afraid of facin folks, of facin the Lord. I done a lot of things I wasn't proud of... sleepin with men after Ed left ... takin up with Charlie ... gittin pregnant when he was married to somebody else. I just couldn't bring myself to walk into a church with all that sin on my shoulders.

Mama had been with us for nearly a year when I hit a wall. I was tense, angry, depressed. Me and Charlie weren't gittin along. If I tried to tell him how tired I was, or how upset Mama made me, he told me it was my own fault, that I needed to leave her on her own, not let her make me her slave.

Maybe he was right. I mean, I did let her walk all over me. And Mama was probably right too. About my needin to give my life back over to the Lord. To quit fightin it and let the Lord show me direction, let Him give me peace. Accordin to her, it was my sins weighin me down and makin me tense. She said I had to lay it all at His feet — ask forgiveness and then accept it.

Some of what I done didn't seem all that sinful. Like divorcin Raymond. Me and the kids might of starved if I stayed with him. The other things, though, I was worried about, and tellin myself I done it all for the kids' sake wasn't true. Some of it had nothin to do with them. I was lonesome and needed somethin for me. I was weak. Maybe bein weak was my biggest sin.

I'd lost the person I thought I was. The person I wanted to be. Some days I was so depressed it was all I could do to git out of bed. If it wasn't for Mama bein there, I wouldn't have. I'd go in her room, and she'd complain about how late I was, about bein left alone so long. And then Charlie'd come at me from the other direction sayin I spent too much time with her. I felt pulled apart.

There was a bottle of whiskey in the cupboard that my brother Laird put there when he was visitin and forgot about. After he left I pushed it behind things so it was hid. I didn't mean to touch it, but I liked knowin it was there. Sometimes I looked at it and put it back where it was. But one day I was really upset and I took a sip. It stung at first, and then there was this warm feelin that I liked, that I remembered from when me and Ed used to go out dancin and he'd buy me drinks. I took another sip, and it made me feel a whole lot better about things. After that I took a drink from time to time. Just one, or maybe two, to git me through the day. And sometimes I'd talk to myself. Not out loud, just in my head.

God damn Charlie. Why can't he see I need help around here? He could wash a dish once in a while. Or go set with Mama. Talk to her. He could help me fix up the house. Git rid of this crappy furniture, these ugly drapes. Throw out his dirty old chair. Buy paint for the walls. Instead he gives me a little money for groceries and pisses the rest away.

Then the bottle'd be empty, and I'd walk to the store. Charlie never paid attention to how I spent the grocery money. Never noticed what I cooked, so I'd git me a bottle of Jim Beam and hide it.

40

WHEN MAMA FIRST CAME, we had four kids at home. Then Sam moved to Modesto and Janie got an apartment with a girlfriend in Sacramento. That left only Eddie and Kathy, and neither of them was around much. Eddie had his after school job and Kathy, well she spent way too much time with her boyfriend. And that was another big worry. She was barely sixteen. Way too young to be serious with a boy. She wouldn't listen to me, though, and I tried to git Charlie to talk to her.

One night I seen this TV program about kids and drugs. Showin how people they called "pushers" hung around schools and got kids to try marijuana. It said once they smoked it, they'd be hooked. They'd go crazy and do all sorts of terrible things. I'd had a little bit to drink, and when Kathy got home I tore into her.

"Where've you been?" I asked. "I don't know where you are half the time."

"I was at Brian's house," she said, squirmin past me to her bedroom.

I followed her. "You spend too much time over

there. You should be here. With your own family."

"Here? Why should I be here? There's nobody around."

"I'm here. Grandma's here."

"But you're not... here!" She waved her arms toward the livin room and kitchen. You're always in there. With Grandma."

"You could come in where we are."

"Oh sure. I could listen to you read the Bible. Or I could watch Lawrence Welk with you. Give me a break."

"You watch your mouth," I said. "What's happened to you? All you do anymore is sass me."

"Mom, it's true. You're always in with Grandma. And Dad's either at work or sleeping. There's no life here. No fun, no conversation, no music. You don't even cook meals anymore." She said she remembered when the other kids were home. How we used to set around the table and eat together. How Rosalie was always cuttin up and makin ever'body laugh. How I used to sing and fool around with em.

"There were fights too," she said, "but even that was better than this. It's like a morgue around here now."

"I don't know where you are or what you do." I said. "How do I know you're not usin marijuana? And you'd better not be drinkin either."

"I'm at Brian's house, that's where I am. With his family. Where they talk to each other. Laugh. Eat together. I'm not using pot. And I'm not drinking. But why shouldn't I? You do. You're drunk half the time."

My hand shot out, and I slapped her.

I stood there, stunned by what I had done. Wishin I could take it back. "Oh honey," I said reachin for her,

"I'm so sorry. I didn't mean…"

She gave me a spiteful look. Said she hated me. Hated the way we lived. She ran out of the house. I was ashamed. Ashamed I slapped her. Ashamed I drank. Ashamed that she knew I drank. I went to the kitchen and poured the rest of the Jim Beam down the sink. Buried the bottle under papers in the trashcan. And promised myself I wouldn't buy any more.

I felt like I was fallin apart. I was havin headaches, night sweats. The doctor said it was nothin to worry about. That I was just goin through the change. The headaches, that was just nerves. He prescribed Valium. Said it would help.

And it did. When I took one, things didn't seem like such a big deal. Mama didn't upset me, and I didn't git so mad at Kathy. Two made me feel good enough to clean my house, do laundry, cook a nice supper.

In November Charlie's boss give him a twenty-pound turkey and I was lookin forward to Thanksgivin, to havin a houseful of people again. The two older boys would be home and Janie was bringin a friend. Eddie had joined the service, so he wouldn't be here, but I'd asked Kathy to invite her boyfriend, Brian.

On Thanksgivin I got up early and took a couple of Valiums. I made the stuffin, got the bird in the oven, and started in on the pies. I had to keep checkin on Mama, and when I started to feel like I was gittin behind, I took a couple more pills.

I don't remember anythin after the pies. The ambulance or the hospital or none of it. Whatever happened was a accident, just a stupid accident, but I scared ever'body. And Kathy stayed mad at me for a long time.

41

I COULDN'T HELP THINKIN Kathy gettin pregnant was my fault. If I'd been a better mother, run a better house, paid more attention to her, to what she was doin, it wouldn't of happened. I thought Charlie would blow up, but he didn't. He just went slack, like all the starch was gone out of him. "Bring Brian over here," he said. "We'll have a talk."

Kathy and Brian stood in our livin room, holdin hands. Kathy's eyes blazed with determination. "Brian's mom didn't freak out," she said. "She's on our side."

"Well so are we," I snapped. "Why would we be against you?"

"Because you always are."

"That's not true and you know it."

"Veda, enough..." Charlie made a quick motion across his throat. He held his breath and let it out with a low whistle. "I know somebody," he said. "He could help you get—"

"No!" Kathy looked like she was goin to cry. "We're not getting rid of it, Dad, if that's what you mean. We want it. We're keeping this baby."

"Don't be stupid. You're kids. You have no idea."

"It's my life, Dad," Kathy said.

Charlie glared at her for a minute. "Well, I guess you'll find out for yourselves. So what do you plan to do?"

"We'll get married," Brian said.

"Okay," Charlie raised his eyebrows, "how…?"

"Lorna … Brian's mom…" Kathy said, "she'll pay for us to fly to Las Vegas."

"That's the least of it," Charlie said. "What will you live on? Do you have any idea what it costs to live … to raise a family?"

"I'll get a job," Brian said. "We'll both get jobs."

"And after the baby comes, then what?" Charlie asked. Nobody spoke for a couple of minutes, and I could tell Kathy was workin up the nerve to say somethin else. She glanced at Brian, then at me. "Mom, you'll have to come to Las Vegas with us. You and Brian's mom. You'll have to sign for us."

"Why Las Vegas? Why not just go to a judge, or have a quiet little weddin here at the house?"

Kathy and Brian looked at each other. "Here? No," Kathy said, "Lorna says there are wedding chapels in Las Vegas that do the flowers and the music and everything. And there's no waiting period. It will be easier that way. You wouldn't have to…"

They had it all figured out. And what else was there to do? Unlike Charlie, I would never suggest they git rid of the baby. Brian was mature for his age, and I suppose Kathy was, too, even though she didn't always act like it. She'd have to quit school, and I regretted that, but the deed was done. My baby was goin to have a baby of her own.

On the airplane, Kathy kept peelin my fingers off her arm, sayin I was makin bruises. My ears popped, wheels hit the ground with a bump, and I couldn't hear what the pilot was tellin us to do. We got off the plane and the heat almost knocked me over. It was the end of August, 1968. Las Vegas must be the hottest place on the face of the earth.

Walkin into the cooled lobby of Caesar's Palace, though, was like walkin into heaven. I looked around and could barely take it all in. The chandeliers, the gold and marble, the statues. I felt like, as Charlie would say, a turd in a punchbowl. The carpet was so thick I practically waded across the lobby to the registration desk. The kid behind it didn't look much older than Brian.

He flashed me a big smile. "Can I help you?"

"I'd like to register."

"All right. One bed or two?"

"Two."

He pushed a heavy book at me and I wrote down my name and address. Then I paid him and he handed me a key.

"That's just one key," I said, puzzled. "I wanted two rooms."

"You said two beds. One room."

"No I didn't. I said I wanted two rooms."

"Ma'am, you said--" He wasn't smilin now.

"Well then, I made a mistake," I said. "I need two rooms. So can I git another one?"

"That was the last one," he said. "We're full."

I stared at him. I didn't believe him for a minute. Place as big as that.

"There are lots of other hotels on the strip. Try one

of those." He shoved my money across the desk and turned his back. I was pissed. I knew how much Kathy and Brian wanted to stay at Caesar's Palace.

"Never mind then," I said. "We'll keep this one."

"Mom," Kathy said when I told her what happened, "it's our wedding night. What were you thinking?"

"It was a mistake," I said, "and I'm sorry."

I knew Kathy thought I'd spoiled ever'thin, but it wasn't like I done it on purpose. Lorna laughed when I told her what had happened and we agreed to find a place in one of the other casinos, but first she wanted to see the kids' room. It was on the fourth floor, at the end of a long hall. None of us could believe how grand it was. All the furniture, includin the beds, was shiny dark wood, carved with swirls and curlicues. The bathroom had tile, and crystal fixtures, and a window over the bathtub that looked out at all of Las Vegas. "It's so fancy," I told Kathy. "I wouldn't be able to sleep in a room like this anyhow."

We took a taxi to the Justice Center, where Kathy and Brian would git a marriage license, and set on a bench with half a dozen other couples. Brian and Kathy were the only kids, ever'body else looked a lot older. When it was their turn, all four of us went up to the window.

"Are you the parents?" the clerk asked. "I'll need to see some I.D."

Lorna pulled out her driver's license and laid it on the counter. Then the man looked at me and said, louder, like maybe I didn't hear him. "YOUR DRIVER'S LICENSE."

"I… I don't have one," I said. "I don't drive."

"Well, ma'am, a passport then. A birth certificate?"

"I don't… I didn't think…"

"Ma'am, I need something to prove who you are. Do you have anything? Something with your name and address on it?"

My stomach knotted up. We'd came all this way, spent all this money, and the kids weren't goin to be able to git married after all. I started to rummage around in my purse. My hands shook so bad I couldn't get hold of anythin, so I dumped my purse on the counter. Lipstick, coins, wadded-up Kleenex. Kathy looked mortified. Finally I found a receipt from the Bible bookstore. It had my name and address on it. The man looked at me like he didn't believe anybody could be so dumb. But he said it would do. I think he just wanted to git rid of me.

The Chapel of the Bells was done up in soft colors, with pews and big baskets of plastic flowers. A little white-haired man greeted us. "I'm Reverend Smalls," he said. Then he pointed at a big woman whose flowery dress made her look like a overstuffed armchair, "and that's the missus over there at the organ."

Brian was in a new blue suit, and Kathy had on a short white dress and a cute little hat with a veil. Standin there, sayin vows, they seemed older than sixteen. They looked so proud and happy that I decided to stop worryin. I told myself they'd be fine and Kathy would git over bein mad at me.

After a nice dinner at one of the Caesar's Palace restaurants, the kids went up to the room and me and Lorna headed for the casino. All the way to Las Vegas Lorna had talked about playin the slots and, with the weddin over with, she wanted to gamble for a while before we went out to look for a room. The smell of cigarette smoke made my head spin, so I set down at the first vacant slot machine. I started winnin right away. Bells went off, nickels flew out and made a awful racket as they hit the pan. It was excitin. I'd win, and then put the nickels back in till I won again. I was havin so much fun I lost track of time. When I finally ran out of nickels, I realized it was way past midnight, and we still had to go out and git a room.

I found Lorna in one of the bars, drunk, with her head on the table, and I set down next to her. *Shit,* I thought, *we can't go out with her in this shape*. Then I noticed ever'body was starin at a television over the bar. The sound was off, but I could tell it was some kind of riot. People runnin ever whichaway. Cops hittin people with clubs, kickin em, draggin em by the hair. It was horrible. I didn't understand what it was all about.

"Democratic Convention," somebody said. "Damn hippies protesting the Vietnam War."

I shook Lorna. "Come on," I said, "we gotta go." I shook her again. I wanted to go tell the kids what was happenin. I thought they needed to know.

I got Lorna to her feet and sort of half-walked, half-dragged her to the elevator and down the long hall. I pounded on the kids' door and it was several minutes before it opened a couple of inches and was stopped by a chain. Kathy peeked out. She looked annoyed. "Mom? What's wrong?"

"Turn on the TV," I said, "you won't believe your eyes."

I was sorry about bargin in on the kids like that, but once they turned on the TV and seen what was happenin, they weren't mad. Lorna laid down on the second bed in the room and went to sleep, while me and Kathy and Brian set watchin that horrible scene play over and over and over. The Vietman War had been on the television news almost every night and Charlie seemed to think it was okay, fightin commies and all that, but I didn't like watchin it and I tried to block it out. Except for Eddie, who was in the Coast Guard, my boys were done with their military service so it hadn't seemed personal to me. But seein this thing, this riot, all these young people... the ones bein made to fight... to git killed for somethin they didn't believe in... made me take notice in a way I hadn't before.

Brian wasn't eighteen yet, but soon he'd be the right age to git drafted. He'd just got married. Had a baby on the way. I could see now how scared he and Kathy were. And I was scared too. For them, for me. I couldn't help but think what a hard time for a young couple to be gettin started. We hadn't talked about none of that before, but we did now. We talked all night. Then the sun come up and we went and had breakfast.

42

I WANT YOU TO TEACH ME to drive," I told Charlie. He had been after me for years, and I put him off. But after the shame of Las Vegas, I wanted a license. For identification, if nothin else. Besides, Kathy was gone now. All the kids were. If I needed to go anywhere, I had to wait on Charlie to take me.

We went to the high school parkin lot and I got in the driver's seat. "Okay now," Charlie said, "put your right foot on the brake and hold down the clutch with your left."

"Which one's the clutch?" I asked.

"It's that one over there, under your left foot."

"Okay. Now what?"

"Turn the key… No, don't grind it, just turn it until the engine starts, and let go. Now put your right foot on the gas pedal. That's the long one."

"But what about the brake? What foot goes on the brake?"

"You'll use the same foot. Real slow now, push on the gas and let the clutch out at the same time."

Soon as I did that, the car jumped like it was tryin to

git out from under me, and died.

"Slowly," Charlie said. "Slow-ly." He let out his breath. "Let's try again."

Finally I got the car movin, but then I was goin way too fast so I stomped on the brake. Charlie sucked his teeth. "Try it again."

We went over to that school three or four different days, and each time Charlie ended up mad, and I ended up cryin. I would of give up altogether if wasn't for Bobby. He was livin in Modesto, but he come over and helped me. He didn't make me nervous the way Charlie did, and I finally got good enough to drive on the street.

I don't know how many fifty-year-olds git their first driver's license, but the examiner that got in the car with me looked surprised.

"All right," he said, holdin his pencil over a clipboard, "are we ready? Go ahead and start the car."

I managed to turn the key and not kill the engine. That was good.

"Pull away from the curb."

I did that.

"You didn't signal." He licked the end of his pencil and made a mark on the paper. "Go to the next corner and make a right."

I had a death grip on the steerin wheel and I was afraid of what'd happen if I let go with one hand. But I had to signal, so I stuck my arm out the window, hand pointin up. The car lurched to the right and almost hit the stop sign. The man licked his pencil again.

I was wet under my arms and my heart was practically jumpin out of my mouth, but I made the corner. I drove for about three blocks before a car come at me from a side street and I stomped on the brake.

"Jesus, lady," the examiner squawked, "you had the right of way. He wasn't going to hit you." Another mark.

Oh shit, I'll never git through this.

"Turn right at the next intersection," he said. "We're going to see you parallel park."

That was somethin I could do. Bobby'd made me practice it over and over till I had it down. *If I can just do this right, maybe he'll forgit about those other things.*

"Okay, stop here. Park between these two cars." It was a good size space, plenty big enough for the Buick. There was a nice high curb with one of them big blue mailboxes on it. I pulled up beside the car in front and backed up till my bumper was even with its door. Then I started turnin the wheel, real sharp like Bobby showed me. *There.* I pushed on the gas. Maybe a little too hard. There was a WHUMP, and a loud scrapin noise.

"Jesus H. Christ, lady! You're half way up the damn mailbox, for God's sake!" He scribbled for a long time and then got out of the car and walked around to the driver's side. He signaled for me to scoot over, and he got in. When we got back to the DMV office, he went over to where Charlie was waitin and handed him the keys.

"He looked kind of shell-shocked," Charlie said on the way to the car. "I guess you didn't pass."

43

As Mama got stronger, she got even harder to deal with. She'd come over to my side of the house and tell me how messy it was. Tell me what to do and how to do it. She complained about germs, said I was goin to make ever'body sick. I found myself thinkin I liked it better when she was bed-ridden. At least then she wasn't checkin up on me all the time.

I wrote to Bea. "You need to take Mama back to Oregon for a while." I said. "I'm not well myself and I need a rest." I was anxious for Mama to be gone, but I knew, in a way, I'd miss her. With her here, I had to be up by a certain time, fix her meals at a certain time, watch TV programs with her at a certain time. Without her, there'd be nothin to shape my day around.

So I put a notice on the bulletin board at the grocery store sayin I wanted to do after-school care. I could watch a couple little kids for a few hours a day till their mothers got off work. It'd give me somethin to do, and we could use the extra money. That's how I got started watchin those two little third-graders, Suzy and JoAnn.

They reminded me of my girls at that age, so full of

life, and I liked havin em around. Charlie got a kick out of em too. He'd tease em and show em things. I thought it was nice. But after a while it started to bother me. The way he was always ticklin and grabbin at em. Then one time I come in the front room and seen Suzy settin on his lap. It give me a bad feelin. I told her to git off, and after the girls went home, I laid into Charlie. "It ain't right," I said. "They're too big to be settin on your lap."

He got mad. Real mad. Just like that time in Central Point. Said I was makin somethin out of nothin and he resented it. After that I let it drop. Told myself I was just bein touchy. But I did keep a closer eye on the girls and I never saw em on his lap again.

Except for those couple hours on school days, it was just me and Charlie at home, and it felt strange. We had never been alone before. There'd always been the kids, and then Mama. But with just the two of us, Charlie started runnin around the house naked, wantin to fuck in the middle of the day. I made excuses, say I had a migraine or I was worried about the little girls walkin in on us if school let out early.

He had let himself go. Put on a lot of weight, and had this smell that hung on him from the cigars he smoked. But that was only part of it. The real problem was what I felt, or rather what I didn't feel. When we weren't gittin along, which was a lot of the time, I didn't want to have sex. I couldn't pretend I liked it. For me, sex had to mean somethin. But I guess it was different for Charlie. He wanted it, and if I put him off, he got mad, accused me of bein frigid like his first wife.

Mama was still in Oregon when Bea called to tell me my brother Laird had been killed. He'd just got out of the sanitarium where he went to cure his alcohol problem, and he had a relapse. Got drunk and was beat up by some thugs. He was found dead on the side of the road. It broke my heart. I loved Laird. He was closer to me than any of my brothers. He'd helped me out so many times over the years. Drove me to the hospital when my babies were born, helped me and Raymond move all them times, and played with my kids when they needed a man in their lives. Even with his drinkin problem, he was always there for me.

And Laird's death just about killed Mama. When Bea brought her back, Mama was usin a walker again and seemed to have aged years instead of months. It wasn't only that Laird was dead, but that he died without bein saved. "The Lord will come callin for you one of these days too, Veda," she told me more than once. "I don't want you to be caught up short the way Laird was."

With Mama grievin the way she was and needin so much care, I had to give up watchin the little girls. Charlie wasn't happy about Mama comin back and he was more peevish than usual. He talked back to the television when somethin provoked him, got riled up over things in the newspaper, complained about work. And when I tried to talk to him, he brushed me off like I was a mere cobweb.

44

COULDN'T OF BEEN MORE than eight o'clock in the mornin when them ladies showed up. I was still in my robe, hair stickin to the side of my head, and I wouldn't of opened the door except I could see who it was through the side window and, well, I just knew it was somethin bad. They both lived on our street. It was their girls I had took care of. They come in, no hello or nothin. "Veda, it's Charlie," one of em said. "He's been doing things…"

I looked from her to the other one. "What things? What do you mean?"

"Showing himself…"

"What? Showin? Showin what?"

"Veda listen. Showing. Exposing himself, his penis."

My legs buckled. I had to set down. "What? To who? Showin it to who?"

"Our girls. He stands out on your back porch and opens his bathrobe when the girls walk by. Our girls, Veda! And he's done it more than once."

There was a roar in my ears. I was scared I'd pass out. I knew he went out on the porch a lot in that ratty old plaid bathrobe of his. Said I kept it too hot in the house. Complained about it. Had to get some air, he said. *Was that what he was doin? No God, please.* My armpits felt clammy. "Why are you sayin this?" It came out a whisper.

"Veda, we're going to the sheriff. We have to. But we wanted to tell you first. It's nothing against you at all. But we have to report him. Do you understand?"

"No. No, I don't understand. Why would he do that? He wouldn't do that. It's gotta be a mistake. The girls, did they say that? Are you sure they said it was him?" I started to cry. "Look, don't go to the police. I'll talk to him. They must of thought they saw —"

"Veda, they saw. These girls are eight years old. Something like this could damage them for life."

I kept shakin my head. My face was wet with tears and snot. One of em handed me a Kleenex. "Veda," she said, "it's not you. It's him. We can't let him keep on hurting children." She bent down and give me a quick hug. Then they left.

I set there cryin, tryin to think. Tryin *not* to think. I didn't know what to do. I didn't know what would happen. Would the sheriff come to the house? Go to Charlie's work? My mind bounced all over the place. I pictured him face down on the floor, in handcuffs. Cops, sirens, bullhorns. Seen him barrin the door, refusin to come out. Like on the TV. I got up and paced, huggin myself to keep my insides from fallin out. *Oh God in heaven*, I thought, *give me the strength to deal with this.* Bad as it was for them girls and their families, it would be a lot worse for ours.

My mind raced. Images roared through it like a freight train. Him walkin around the house naked. Him with his bathrobe just barely closed. Goin out on the back porch. Takin those little girls out to his shop to show em things. Holdin em on his lap...

I tried to pull myself together and went to look in on Mama. She was settin on the edge of her bed. "What took you so long?" she asked. "I need my bath."

I filled the tub and checked the water temperature with my elbow, the way I always done for my babies, and helped her in. Then I soaped up a washrag and started scrubbin her back.

"Not so hard," she said pullin away. "What's wrong with you?" She turned to look at me. "There's something wrong, isn't there? What is it?"

I dropped the washrag, leaned over to close the toilet lid, and set down on it.

"Come on," she said, "spit it out."

I put my head in my hands and started to bawl. I tried to talk, but I couldn't.

"Okay," she said. "Take a deep breath. Tell me."

"It's... Mama... It's Charlie," I stammered. "They say he's been... Oh God, Mama, they say he's been exposin himself."

"Who says? Who told you this?"

"They come here to the house. Said they were goin to the police."

"Who, Veda?"

"Eleanor and Betty. Said it was their girls. Those two I watched while you were gone. That little Suzy with the pigtails and the Burns girl."

"Little girls make up things," Mama said. "It's best the police are in on it. They'll find out if it's true or not."

"But what am I goin to do? I can't act like nothin's happened."

"Veda," Mama said, "what you do is you go in there

and clean house. Bake somethin. Start supper. Do whatever it takes to keep busy. What happens happens. He'll be cleared. Wait and see."

Mama was willin to give Charlie the benefit of the doubt. I wanted to, but I kept thinkin about that little girl settin on his lap. About the thing in Central Point when them other girls accused him. Mama said to keep busy, bake. How could I do that? I couldn't even think straight. My feet felt like cast iron skillets. I went back and forth through the house, pickin things up from one place and layin em down someplace else.

I put on a pot of beans, folded a few pieces of laundry from the pile on the couch. What would I say to him when he got home? If he got home. Should I warn him or just keep quiet and wait for the police to come? I was afraid to face him, to tell him. Afraid of how mad he'd be.

The clock ticked off the minutes. The hours. I could smell my sweat. Two or three times I went and soaped up a washrag and scrubbed under my arms. I wanted the day to be over, but at the same time I dreaded it. He would come home and want me to pay attention to him. I made coffee. He always liked to have coffee first thing.

It was a little after six o'clock when I heard the car, and then Charlie, gruntin and puffin as he come up on the porch. I always figured he did that so I'd see how tired he was, know how hard he worked. I checked the stove, the beans looked done. I made myself busy washin dishes I should of done hours ago. Buyin time. I couldn't look at him. He would see I was upset. "What now?" he'd say.

From the front room where he took his coffee, he was tellin about one of his co-workers doin somethin or other. Hurtin himself, and how it was the guy's own fault. Then a sheriff's car pulled up and parked in front of the house. Charlie went to the door. Two uniformed men were on the porch.

"Mr. Steele," they said flashin their badges, "we've had a report..."

It took all the money I could scrape together. What I had put away for groceries and what Mama give me from her Social Security to help out. Walkin into that sheriff's office to bail out my husband was one of the most humiliatin things I ever had to do. The way the deputy looked at me made me ashamed. If Charlie'd been took in for drunk drivin or stealin or just about any other thing, I could of stood it. Maybe even if he killed somebody. I don't know. I suppose it would depend on why. But there wasn't no excuse for this. He come out and made a beeline for the taxi I had waitin. Neither one of us said a word on the ride home.

I stayed up half the night starin at the TV without any idea what was on. Charlie hollered, "Come to bed," but I couldn't bear the thought of sleepin with him. When I couldn't keep my eyes open anymore, I went in one of the empty bedrooms and curled up on top of the blankets.

The newspaper report stirred up a shitstorm. Girls that hadn't spoke up before said Charlie had done worse things than just showin his pecker. They said he touched em, fondled em, made em promise not to tell.

Kathy phoned, cryin. Brian's mom had seen it in the paper and called her. "It isn't true, is it, Mom? How could he do this? And why did I have to hear about it this way?"

I didn't know what to say to her, or anyone else. I stayed in the house so I wouldn't have to face the neighbors. The girls' families said they wouldn't press charges if Charlie pled guilty to indecent exposure and left town. He was told to sell the house, settle his business, and leave. He would git off easy. No jail time.

Charlie went around with a black cloud over his head, and I went around in a cold sweat. He refused to own up to any of it. Claimed the girls lied. For a month he set on his hands, growlin about bein tarred and feathered. He wouldn't put the house up for sale and wouldn't go down to the court to sign the papers to keep himself out of jail. He kept talkin about gittin a lawyer, but didn't do that either. He got fired from his job, so we were goin to lose the house anyhow. I didn't know where we'd go or what we'd live on. Neither one of us was old enough to git Social Security. And it was a sure bet I wouldn't git any more babysettin jobs.

45

MAMA HAD BEEN ON Charlie's side at first, but after them other things come out, them other little girls, she said she couldn't bear it. Bea drove down again to git her and they left without sayin anythin to Charlie. I thought of goin back to Oregon with em, but my kids were all in California and I didn't want to be that far away. After Mama left, I moved into her rooms and listened to Charlie through the walls. Stompin around, bangin things, swearin from time to time. Carryin on like it was him that was wronged instead of them girls.

Finally, he agreed to register as a sex offender, and we signed a quitclaim deed on the house. The whole business made me sick. I felt like I been stuck in quicksand my whole life. Ever'time I got one leg out, the other one sunk in. Anger stuck in my throat like food that wouldn't go down. As if what he done to them girls wasn't bad enough, he caused us to lose the house too. The house my family had give us the down payment for. I prayed I could find it in me to forgive Charlie, for what he done to them little girls and what he done to me.

"You're not staying with him?" Kathy shouted into the phone. "After what he did?"

"Well, what else can I do? None of you kids want me movin in with you. And I wouldn't do that to you anyway. I know how hard that is on a family. On a marriage. This is my problem and I'll figure it out."

"You could —"

"I could what? I don't have any money of my own. I don't have any skills. Hell, I can't even pass a goddamn driver's test."

"You can't stay."

"Well I'm goin to. Charlie's lookin for a house to rent, and I'll go wherever that is."

Charlie got a part-time job up in the hills towards Reno and rented a little two-bedroom cabin. The move was hard with just the two of us wrestlin furniture, luggin boxes, and goin back to clean the empty house. Charlie said to leave it, but I wouldn't. The neighbors would have enough to gossip about. I didn't want em sayin I left a filthy house too.

I unpacked at the new place. Put away dishes and books and clothes. Hung up the kids' graduation pictures the way I had em in the other house. I was so proud of them pictures, but there was only six, not seven. Kathy had went on and got her diploma after she was married, but she didn't git a picture made.

It was hot and I was dead tired. I told Charlie I'd be takin the back bedroom, and he didn't argue. For days I dragged around tryin to put the place in order, and went to bed soon as supper was over. I couldn't put what Charlie done out of my mind. Carryin it weighed me down and all I wanted to do was sleep.

We put the electric and phone services in my name 'cause Charlie's was on the unpaid bills at the old address. I got a checkin account in my name too, and took over payin the bills, promisin myself we wouldn't git behind ever again.

I liked bein in the woods. It was peaceful and quiet and there was all that clean, piney air. Made me think of the campin trips we used to take with the kids, and how much I used to love to fish. I rummaged around in our shed and found a pole and a reel and decided to give it a try. I went most mornins after that. Dug up some worms, took a thermos of coffee and a sandwich and set by the river. Sometimes I caught a couple of rainbow trout, but if I didn't, that was okay too.

It's funny how things stick in your mind. I read somethin once about buryin your troubles. Just diggin a hole and buryin em. It sounded silly, but I was diggin up worms anyway. So I dug way down deep, to where the bottom of the hole was startin to fill up with river water. I got me a rock and threw it in the hole. *Okay*, I thought, *I'm goin to let it go. It's Charlie's sin, not mine.* Then I pushed all the dirt back in and covered up the hole. It was such a ridiculous thing to do, but it made me feel better somehow. And when Charlie started comin along with me to the river on his days off, I didn't mind so much. We just set quiet, watchin the water rush past our lines, only talkin when one of us got a strike.

As time passed, that thing with Charlie got shoved aside. Not forgot about, but not talked about either. He'd swore he hadn't done what they said, that he'd only signed the papers to git the law off his back. I wanted to believe it. I wanted to put the whole mess behind us. The kids all knew Charlie'd lost his job, but nobody questioned why. Kathy knew, but whether the older ones did or not, I couldn't say. It was a shameful thing, and I wasn't goin to be the one to tell em.

46

MAMA GOT BAD AGAIN after she went back to Oregon, and Bea couldn't deal with her. "Can you and Charlie take her back?"

"We don't have room, Bea, you know that. Can't you find a nursin home?"

"Veda, she hates nursing homes. She says she'd rather die."

"They're not all bad," I said. "There's no way I can keep her here."

"Well maybe you could find one where you are. And with you close by, she might not fight it so hard."

"I don't know of any, Bea. But I guess I can look around."

I went through the phone book and made a list. Charlie drove and we spent a whole day visitin foster care and nursin homes. Some were awful. Even dressed up with fancy settin rooms and nice furniture, they smelled like sickness and Lysol and shit. But by the end of the day, I found one that was clean and comfortable without all the window dressin. And the people that run it seemed down-to-earth and genuine. I told em about Mama and how she could be difficult at times. That she would put up a fuss. They said they were used to that, but most folks adjust.

Bea drove Mama down and we got her settled in. I knew I'd have to pass the driver's test and git me a car so I could visit Mama without Charlie havin to take me, so I started lookin for ads in the paper and found a used Ford Pinto. Charlie drove it and said, except for the dent in the fender, it was in good shape. Once I got it, I couldn't wait to git my license. This time a lady officer give me the test. She was friendly and didn't make me nervous. Just got in the car like me and her was goin for a Sunday drive. Said to turn here, and go there, and I didn't make no mistakes at all. When she told me I passed, I was so tickled I hugged her.

I drove all over the place in that little green car. Grocery store, the bank, and up to the post office. I wasn't brave enough to go to the city, but around them quiet streets where we lived was easy, and I felt proud of myself. I went to see Mama every day. Set in her room, ate with her, read to her, brushed her hair, and made sure she got her medicines on time. When she dozed off, I wandered around and did what I could to help with the other old people. Got to know all their names, and ever'time I come out of Mama's room, one or more of em was waitin for me, wantin my attention.

Of course, I had my favorites. Mary was near ninety. She had this baby-doll that she carried around all the time, talked to it like it was real. But Mary could still play the piano, and when she set down to play you'd swear you was listenin to Liberace. And there was Bert, a cute little man with a sweet disposition. Bent over he wasn't more'n five feet tall. He fancied himself a ladies' man and he kept the staff busy makin sure he wasn't climbin in bed with his favorites.

Mama didn't like the nurses, the food, or her room, and she didn't like bein penned up with a bunch of "lunatics." She might of been easier to deal with if she was senile, but she wasn't. The only one she liked in the whole place was the young Adventist minister that come every Sabbath to visit her. She was gettin real frail, and I didn't know how much longer I'd have her.

On her ninetieth birthday I threw her a party at our place in the woods. We set up a big table on the lawn. Got a sheet cake from the bakery. Had lemonade and balloons, and Mama got lots of cards. Kathy's family was there, and Janie, and Eddie and his wife. Rosalie and Pete drove all the way down from Winslow with their kids. Some of the staff from the nursin home came too, and Mama's minister friend.

There was a nice write-up in the local newspaper about it. Mentioned where Mama grew up, and how many children, grandchildren, and great grandchildren she had. Even put in one of her poems that'd been published in the Adventist magazine, *Review and Herald*. I think that was the part she liked best.

47

MAMA HUNG ON FOR THREE more years. After she passed away, time stretched out like a road to no place. I felt lost, slept late, and didn't know what to do with myself. The only thing I ever done in my life was take care of people, and with Mama gone, there wasn't nobody to take care of. The kids were all grown up. None of my grandkids lived close. And I was sure as hell done takin care of Charlie.

I missed Mama. Missed all those old people at the nursin home. So after a time I started goin back. The nurses told me what would help most was to set with folks. Just hold their hands and listen to em talk. They were lonesome, and most of em didn't have family come visit like I done with Mama. So that's what I did. I listened. And what I heard from a lot of em was how scared they was of dyin. Not the pain or what they was leavin behind, but scared of what would happen to em after. Scared of goin to Hell. It didn't seem right. Seemed to me if they done things they was sorry for, things like hurtin somebody, or havin a hateful heart, they could make peace with God on their own, and they didn't need a preacher to set there and hear em say it. So I held their hands and told em they didn't need to be afraid. Told em God loves all his children and nothin bad was gonna happen.

But in truth, I was scared too. All my life, Mama had pounded fear into me the same way she pounded dirt out of Papa's overalls. Told me over and over that I had to be ready, to make sure my slate was clean. But my ears was so stopped up with resentment about how the church had treated me, that I refused to listen. I hadn't ever stopped believin in Jesus. Believin that there was a God and a heaven. I always knew God was watchin over me and my kids, always knew He'd forgive me for the things I done if only I asked Him in my heart. I just didn't like havin Mama's style of religion shoved down my throat.

What I was tellin the old folks brought me around to askin for forgiveness for my own sins. But it says in the Lord's Prayer, "Forgive us our trespasses as we forgive those who trespass against us," so I knew I had to go first. I had to forgive the people who had wronged me, and that was the hard part. I wondered if I would be able to do it.

I set in the parkin lot of the local Adventist Church with a dry mouth and a gut knotted up like a piece of cheap rope. I knew I could of gone to a different kind of church, but I had tried before. There was somethin about all of em that didn't fit, and I realized that the first step in the forgivin process was to make peace with the church that had banished me. The church I'd tried so hard to run away from.

I took a deep breath, clamped my purse so tight under my arm it had to be leavin red marks, and got out of the car.

Inside, the organist was playin "Rock of Ages … Cleft for me, Let me hide myself in thee," a song that'd always been my favorite. People smiled and shook my hand, and I settled into a pew to listen. The words were familiar but, at the same time, different. Where I would of heard judgment before, now I heard love. Love and hope and forgiveness. It was on people's faces. In their gestures. Shinin in through the windows. And when ever'body stood up to sing, I did too. I didn't even need a hymnbook.

I went back the next week, and the next, lookin forward to it ever'time. I could feel my heart open up and let go of all that stuff from the past, all those old resentments. I forgave Raymond and his mother, the Grants Pass church, and them ladies in the Dorcas Society.

Ed was another matter entirely. Somethin I'd never come to grips with. I suppose I forgave him too, even though I half believed there was nothin to forgive. Maybe him disappearin wasn't his fault. Maybe he did drown. Or if he did run off, maybe he had a reason. I still loved him, or at least I loved his memory, so I made allowances.

Gittin rid of all that bitterness and hurt shifted somethin inside me, and I knew it was time to ask the Lord to forgive me. So I stayed in the pew one Sabbath after ever'body was gone, and I talked to God. I told him how sorry I was for all the wrong things I done. For sleepin with those men after Ed left, for takin up with Charlie when he was married to someone else, for the drinkin, and for takin His name in vain. I asked him to forgive me for the hateful thoughts and grudges I held against people, and for placin so much blame on

Him for things that happened. I got down on my knees then, and asked him for ... what was the word Raymond used? Redemption.

There was a real difference in me after that. The tension in my shoulders was gone and I could walk into a room without feelin nervous or guarded. And without feelin ashamed. I even joined the Dorcas Society. It made me feel useful. I helped collect clothes for families in the kinds of straits I was in when my kids was little. I knitted hats and scarves for homeless people, and worked at the food bank. Before long I was doin things I'd always been too shy to do, like speakin in front of people and takin charge of rummage sales.

After a while Charlie started comin to church with me. He drove, of course, 'cause he never did git over me messin up so bad on that first driver test. A church can always use a big strong man who can fix plumbin and paint classrooms. They even give him the job of keepin the church's books and payin the bills. I thought that was funny, seein as how he never did a decent job handlin money of his own.

48

I WOKE UP ON THE KITCHEN floor. Charlie was bent over me sayin my name.

"Oh God," I moaned. "What happened?"

"You passed out."

There was a funny taste in my mouth, like … pennies. "I was dizzy, queasy. I saw a blindin light and then ever'thin went black."

"I heard you hit the floor," Charlie said. "When I came in here you were flopping around like a catfish."

The headaches had got worse. Sometimes I thought the top of my head was goin to come off. I'd been to the doctor several times, but he didn't find anythin serious. Just told me it was common for ladies in their late fifties to have headaches. He give me pills. Over-the-counter ones at first, like Excedrin, then ones I had to have a prescription for. None of em helped much. I stopped tellin Charlie about the headaches 'cause he tended not to believe me. But I never blacked out before.

Charlie told me to stay put, that a ambulance was on the way. I could tell he was scared. He rode in the ambulance with me and waited at the hospital the whole time while a couple different doctors checked me out. Then I heard em in the hallway talkin to Charlie. It was a seizure, they said, and they were sendin me to Sacramento to git some tests done.

It was a Monday, and the city traffic made Charlie fume. He yelled at a guy for not lettin him in the lane he needed, and he yelled at me when he missed the exit. The medical center was huge. Lots of floors and elevators and confusin signs. When we got to the right office, the girl at the desk said, "You're late," real snotty. I started to tell her we never been there before, but she just pushed a clipboard at me and said, "Fill this out. We'll call you when it's your turn." Then after her bein so snippy with me for bein late, I had to set there for nearly a hour before she called my name.

They took me to a room and handed me a gown and told me to take off ever'thin but my underpants. Then they give me a shot and rolled me up to a machine that looked like a huge doughnut. The test itself was short, but the drive there and all the rigmarole gittin the paperwork filled out and waitin my turn took the whole day. We ended up eatin supper in the hospital cafeteria. And that was just the first test. They told me to come back the next week for another test in a new kind of machine.

After that it was two terrible weeks of waitin and worryin before my next appointment. Either they'd tell me nothin was wrong, and I knew there was, or else say it was somethin bad. Either way, it wouldn't be good.

The doctor came around the desk and patted me on the

shoulder. "Veda, it's a tumor, a growth, on your brain. That's what's been causing your headaches."

I stared at him and my first thought was, Now Charlie will have to believe me.

"You'll need surgery," he said. "I want you to see a specialist in San Francisco."

I don't know what went through Charlie's mind on the way home, but I was tryin to think of how I was goin to tell the kids. What would I say, "Hi, it's me, I have a brain tumor?"

I was on the phone with Rosalie. "Charlie always said it was all in my head," I laughed.

"Mom," she said, "it's not funny!"

"Well, of course not. But I'm just glad they found somethin. They been puttin me off for years, sayin there wasn't nothin wrong. Sayin I was goin through the change, or it was migraines, or ju

st a case of nerves. Now at least they believe me."

Once the ball got rollin, Charlie took over, makin my appointments, gittin my medicines, and arrangin for the operation. We met with the surgeon, who drew a picture on his prescription pad of how he would cut a hole in my head and go in there and take the thing out. He made it look simple enough. Said they would put me under so I wouldn't feel a thing.

"What then?" I asked.

"First, we'll operate," he said, "then we'll see."

They give me a date, and as the time got closer, the kids come to visit a few at a time. I could see how worried they were, and I kept tellin em I'd be fine. They brought things for me to take to the hospital, books and magazines, hand lotion, crossword puzzle books. It was real sweet, but the attention made me jittery, like they were thinkin it was more serious than they let on. And what if it was?

It was dark outside, but the hospital was lit up like summer. White walls, white tile floor, white window shades, even the plastic chairs in the waitin room was white. At the admissions desk they give me a whole bunch more forms to sign, sayin I give em permission to do it and sayin I understood there was a risk I could die.

"Charlie," I said, "I'm not even sixty years old yet."

"Go ahead and sign," he said. "It's just a formality."

They come and got me with a wheelchair, took me to a little room with a curtain and give me a gown to put on. It was blue with little green and purple triangles on it. "Good," I said, "it's not white." For some reason that little bit of color made me feel better. The nurse left Charlie to help me git undressed. He put my clothes in the drawstring bag they give us, and then the nurse poked her head back in.

"Are we ready? I'm goin to start your IV now," she said. "This will relax you. When we get you into the other room, they'll put you to sleep and you won't feel a thing. When you wake up it'll be all over."

When I came to, my head felt heavy and dull. There was tubes in my arms and nose, and my mouth felt like it was full of cotton. I opened my eyes just enough to see Charlie and Rosalie and Pete beside the bed.

"You did fine, Mom," Rosalie was sayin. "You're going to be fine." They left and the others come in a couple at a time. All talkin soft and sayin they loved me and to get some rest, and then I got real woozy.

The pain came and went. When it got unbearable, a

nurse gave me a shot and I went all woozy again. Hurt and sleep. Hurt and sleep. If I ate or peed or had a bowel movement, I didn't know it. It might of been hours, it might of been days, before I saw the doctor that operated on me. He stood at the foot of my bed.

"Veda," he said, "I'm Dr. Jamison. We did a biopsy on the tumor. It's cancer."

"It's cancer." That's how he said it. Not "I am so sorry," or "I hate to have to tell you this," just, "It's cancer."

I had thought about it, told myself I wouldn't be surprised if I had it, but hearin him say that word, just matter of fact like that, was like gittin kicked in the teeth.

49

WE RENTED A ROOM near the medical center in
Sacramento where my treatments were. The
radiation was easy enough. I went in and got on a table
under a big machine and it just took a few minutes. But
the chemo was somethin else. It made me feel like shit.
Throwin up, diarrhea. Nasty taste in my mouth. It'd be
like that for five or six days, and just about the time I
started to feel like I was goin to live, it was time for the
next go-round. I kept thinkin it didn't make sense to
make a body this sick on purpose. It felt more like they
was tryin to kill me than make me well. When the
doctors seen how bad off I was, they stopped the
chemo, said I needed to go home and rest, gain back
some weight before I started treatments again.

Eddie and his wife bought us a cute little forty-two-
foot singlewide in a nice park on the river. He'd always
hated how Charlie messed things up and he thought a
trailer-house would be easy for him to keep clean. It
was just the right size for two people. Had pretty
wallpaper and a sunny kitchen with one of them new-

fangled microwave ovens that cooked things in no time at all. And there was a deck on the back that run the whole length of the house. It'd be a perfect place to set and drop my fishin line right down in the river. And I was plannin to do just that. Soon as I got well.

Charlie got a hospital bed and set it up in the front room by the windows so I could see out. I stayed there all day, restin and watchin the hummin birds that come to feed at the red plastic thingies Charlie hung up all along the deck. The days went by in a blur. Charlie got a microwave cookbook and tried to tempt me with things, but I couldn't eat. Ever'thin tasted like metal. I had sores in my mouth. It even hurt to drink water.

And it wasn't long before the place was a mess. Stuff piled up. Dirty dishes. Laundry. A film of dust coated the furniture and unopened mail set on a table near my bed, red ink screamin "PAST DUE." Sick as I was, I couldn't help worryin about the bills. I had us all caught up before I got sick, and Charlie'd let it all go to hell.

When the doctor put me back on the chemo, I threw up a dozen times a day. I got down to eighty pounds and I told Charlie I couldn't do it any more. He begged me to keep goin, said he knew I was goin to git better. I knew I wasn't. I knew I was dyin, and dyin was better than livin like this.

I thought a lot about dyin and I thought about Mama. And how, when she was in the nursin home, she talked about goin to heaven and seein Jesus. She said she was ready, that she'd made her peace with God. She used to tell me she hoped she would see me "on the other side." She was ninety-three years old and I was in my early fifties then. I thought I had another thirty years or more.

I keep hearin a song in my head. One that Mama loved.
Safe in the arms of Jesus, safe on His gentle breast,
There by His love o'ershaded, sweetly my soul shall rest.
Hark! 'tis the voice of angels, borne in a song to me.
Over the fields of glory, over the jasper sea.

Mama always told me to make peace with Jesus, and I have. I'm not afraid to die. I expect it'll be like lettin myself fall asleep when I'm bone tired and tryin my damnedest to stay awake.

I believe I will rest in Jesus' arms. And I expect to see Mama, there on the other side, and maybe Laird will be there too. Mama said he wasn't saved but she couldn't know what was in his heart. And I pray that Ed will be there, standin beside Mama, all the bitterness between em gone.

They say when a person is drownin, their whole life flashes in front of their eyes. It's like that now: There's me, young, skinny, workin at them peoples' house and meetin Raymond. There's him and me married and livin in one dump after another. There's my sweet babies. And the Burrises that were so good to me. My "accident," and the divorce. And there! The hardest thing I ever went through. Ed goin off that day, and me never findin out what happened to him. Havin to hear all those things that was said, that he didn't love me or didn't want the responsibility. All those years of missin him, cryin over him, and seein his babies grow up without ever knowin their daddy. Eddie, with the same smile, same blue eyes. Janie, with his tallness, his slender build. Then there's me gittin mixed up with Charlie and movin to California. The fire, the ranch, the kids growin up and leavin home. And all that other stuff. The stuff Charlie's goin to have to atone for.

I feel a sense of peace and a sense of pride. In spite of ever'thin that happened, I had a lot of joy in my life, and the biggest joy of all was seein my kids grow up and become the wonderful people they are. I wish I could see my grandkids grow up, too, but I don't have the strength for this battle anymore. All I want is to lay here and listen to the river. And watch the hummin birds flittin around, backwards and forwards, flashin their bright reds and blues and greens. Charlie says the wings on those tiny things can beat seventy times a second. Isn't that amazin?

THE END

ABOUT THE AUTHOR

Ellen Gardner grew up in the Pacific Northwest and is one of the seven children born to Veda, the protagonist of this book. A photographer as well as a writer, she lives with her husband in Southern Oregon and dotes on her extended family, especially her two newest grand-children.

17934922R00140

Made in the USA
Charleston, SC
07 March 2013